I0634788

George Manville Fenn

**Of High Descent**

A Novel: Vol. I.

George Manville Fenn

**Of High Descent**
*A Novel: Vol. I.*

ISBN/EAN: 9783337065997

Printed in Europe, USA, Canada, Australia, Japan

Cover: Foto ©Andreas Hilbeck / pixelio.de

More available books at **www.hansebooks.com**

# OF HIGH DESCENT.

## A Novel.

BY

## GEORGE MANVILLE FENN,

AUTHOR OF "THIS MAN'S WIFE," ETC.

## *IN THREE VOLUMES.*

## VOL. I.

London:

## WARD AND DOWNEY,

12, YORK STREET, COVENT GARDEN.

1889.

*[All Rights reserved.]*

# CONTENTS OF VOLUME I.

# OF HIGH DESCENT.

## CHAPTER I.

### " IN THE WEST COUNTREE."

" TAKE care, Mr. Luke Vine, sir. There's a big one coming."

The thin, little, sharp-featured, gray-haired man on a rock looked sharply round, saw the " big one coming," stooped, picked up a large basket, and, fishing-rod in hand, stepped back and climbed up a few feet, just as a heavy swell, which seemed to glide along rapidly over the otherwise calm sea, heaved, flooded the rock on which he had been standing, ran right up so high as to bathe his feet, then sank back in a series of glittering falls which sparkled in the glorious sunshine ; there was a hissing and sighing and sucking noise among the rocks, and the wave passed on along the rugged coast, leaving the sea calm and bright once more.

"Many a poor lad's been took like that, Mr. Luke, sir," said the speaker, "and never heard of again. Why, if I hadn't called out, it would have took you off your legs, and the current's so strong here you'd have been swept away."

"And there'd been an end of me, Polly, and nobody a bit the worse, eh?"

The last speaker seemed to fill his sharp, pale face full of tiny wrinkles, and reduced his eyes to mere slits, as he looked keenly at the big robust woman at his side. She was about fifty, but with her black hair as free from gray as that of a girl, her dark eyes bright, and her sun-tanned face ruddy with health, as she bent forward with a great fish-basket supported on her back by means of a broad leather strap passed over her print sun-bonnet and across her forehead.

"Nobody the worse, Mr. Luke, sir?" cried the woman. "What a shame to talk like that! You arn't no wife, nor no child, but there's Miss Louise."

"Louisa, woman, Louisa," said the fisher sharply.

"Well, Louisa, sir. I only want to be right; but it was only yes'day as old Miss

Vine, as stood by when I was selling her some hake, shook her finger at me and said I was to say Miss Louise."

"Humph! Never mind what my sister says. Christened Louisa.—That ought to fetch 'em."

"Yes, sir; that ought to fetch 'em," said the woman in a sing-song way, as the elderly man gave the glistening bait at the end of his running line a deft swing and sent it far out into the bright sea. "I've seen the water boiling sometimes out there with the bass leaping and playing. What, haven't you caught none, sir?"

"No, Polly, not one; so just be off about your business, and don't worry me with your chatter."

"Oh, I'm a-going, sir," said the woman good-humouredly; "only I see you a-fishing, and said to myself, 'Maybe Mr. Luke Vine's ketched more than he wants, and he'd like to sell me some of 'em for my customers.'"

"And I haven't seen a bass this morning, so be off."

"Toe be sure, Mr. Luke Vine, sir; and when are you going to let me come up and give your place a good clean? I says to my 'Liza up at your brother's, sir, only yes'-day——"

"Look here, Polly Perrow," cried the fisher viciously, "will you go, or must I?"

"Don't be criss-cross, sir, I'm going," said the woman, giving her basket a hitch. "Here's Miss Louise—isa—coming down the rocks with Miss Madlin."

"Hang her confounded chatter!" snarled the fisher, as he drew out his bait, unwound some more line, and made another throw, "bad as those wretched stamps."

He cast an angry glance up at the mining works high on the cliff-side, whose chimney shaft ran along the sloping ground till it reared itself in air on the very top of the hill, where in constant repetition the iron-shod piles rose and fell, crushing the broken ore to powder. "A man might have thought he'd be free here from a woman's tongue."

He gave another glance behind him, along the rocky point which jutted out several hundred yards, and formed a natural breakwater to the estuary, which ran, rock-sheltered, right up into the land, and on either side of which were built rugged flights of natural steps, from the bright water's edge to where, five hundred feet above, the gray wind-swept masses of granite looked jagged against the sky.

Then he watched his great painted float,

as it ran here and there in the eddies of the tremendous Atlantic currents which swept along by the point. The sea sparkled, the sun shone, and the gray gulls floated above the deep blue transparent water, uttering a querulous cry from time to time, and then dipping down at the small shoals of fry which played upon the surface.

Far away seaward a huge vessel was going west, leaving behind a trail of smoke; on his right a white-sailed yacht or two glistened in the sun. In another direction, scattered here and there, brown-sailed luggers were passing slowly along; while behind the fisher lay the picturesque straggling old town known as East and West Hakemouth, with the estuary of the little river pretty well filled with craft, from the fishing luggers and trawlers up to the good-sized schooners and brigs which traded round the coast or adventured across the Bay of Storms, by Spain and through the Straits, laden with cargoes of pilchards for the Italian ports.

"Missed him," grumbled the fisher, withdrawing his line to re-bait with a pearly strip of mackerel. "Humph! now I'm to be worried by those chattering girls."

The worry was very close at hand, for directly after, balancing themselves on the rough rocks, and leaping from mass to mass, came two bright-looking girls of about twenty, their faces flushed by exercise, and more than slightly tanned by the strong air that blows health-laden from the Atlantic.

As so often happens in real life as well as in fiction, the companions were dark and fair ; and as they came laughing and talking, full of animation, looking a couple of as bonny-look-ing English maidens as the West Country could produce, their aspect warranted, in reply to the greetings of " Ah, Uncle Luke ! " " Ah, Mr. Vine ! " something a little more courteous than—

" Well, Nuisance ? " addressed with a short nod to the dark girl in white serge, and " Do, Madelaine ? " to the fair girl in blue.

The gruffness of the greeting seemed to be taken as a matter of course, for the girls seated themselves directly on convenient masses of rock, and busied themselves in the govern-ance of sundry errant strands of hair which were playing in the breeze.

The elderly fisher watched them furtively, and his sour face seemed a little less grim, and as if there was something after all pleasant to look upon in the bright youthful countenances before him.

"Well, uncle, how many fish?" said the dark girl.

"Bah! and don't chatter, or I shall get none at all. How's dad?"

"Quite well. He's out here somewhere."

"Dabbling?"

"Yes."

The girl took off her soft yachting cap, and fanned her face; then ceased, and half closing her eyes and throwing back her head, let her red lips part slightly as she breathed in full draughts of the soft western breeze.

"If he ever gives her a moment's pain," said the old man to himself, as he jerked a look up at the mining works, "I'll kill him." Then, turning sharply to the fair girl, he said aloud—"Well, Madelaine, how's the *bon père?*"

"Quite well, and very busy seeing to the lading of the *Corunna,*" said the girl with animation.

"Humph! Old stupid. Worrying himself to death money-grubbing. Here, Louie, when's that boy going back to his place?"

"To-morrow, uncle."

"Good job too. What did he want with a holiday? Never did a day's work in his life. Here! Hold her, Louie. She's going to peck," he added in mock alarm, and with a cynical sneering laugh, as he saw his niece's companion colour slightly, and compress her lips.

"Well, it's too bad of you, uncle. You are always finding fault about Harry."

"Say Henri, pray, my child, and with a good strong French accent," cried the old man, with mock remonstrance. "What would Aunt Marguerite say?"

"Aunt Margaret isn't here, uncle," cried the girl merrily; "and it's of no use for you to grumble and say sour things, because we know you by heart, and we don't believe in you a bit."

"No," said the fisherman grimly, "only hate me like poison, for a sour old crab. Never gave me a kiss when you came."

"How could I, without getting wet?" said the girl, with a glance at the tiny rock island on which the fisher stood.

"Humph! Going back to-morrow, eh? Good job too. Why, he has been a whole half-year in his post."

"Yes, uncle, a whole half-year!"

"And never stayed two months before at any of the excellent situations your father and

I worried ourselves and our friends to death to get for him."

"Now, uncle——"

"A lazy, thoughtless, good-for-nothing young vag—— There, hold her again, Louie. She's going to peck."

"And you deserve it, uncle," cried the girl, with a smile at her companion, in whose eyes the indignant tears were rising.

"What! for speaking the truth, and trying to let that foolish girl see my lord in his right colours?"

"Harry's a good affectionate brother, and I love him very dearly," said Louise, firmly; "and he's your brother's son, uncle, and in your heart you love him too, and you're proud of him as proud can be."

"You're a silly young goose, and as feather-brained as he is. Proud of him? Bah! I wish he'd enlist for a soldier, and get shot."

"For shame, uncle!" cried Louise indignantly; and her face flushed too as she caught and held her companion's hand.

"Yes. For shame! It's all your aunt's doing, stuffing the boy's head full of fantastic foolery about his descent, and the disgrace of trade. And now I am speaking, look here," he cried, turning sharply on the fair girl, and

holding his rod over her as if it were a huge
stick which he was about to use. "Do you
hear, Madelaine?"

"I'm listening, Mr. Vine," said the girl,
coldly.

"I've known you ever since you were two
months old, and your silly mother must insist
upon my taking hold of you—you miserable
little bit of pink putty, as you were then, and
fooled me into being godfather. How I could
be such an ass, I don't know—but I am, and
I gave you that silver cup, and I've wanted it
back ever since."

"Oh, uncle, what a wicked story!" cried
Louise, laughing.

"It's quite true, miss. Dead waste of
money. It has never been used, I'll swear."

"No, Mr. Vine, never," said Madelaine,
smiling now.

"Ah, you need not show your teeth at me
because you're so proud they're white. Lots
of the fisher-girls have got better. That's
right, shut your lips up, and listen. What
I've got to say is this: if I see any more of
that nonsense there'll be an explosion."

"I don't know what you mean," said Madelaine, colouring more deeply.

"Yes you do, miss. I saw Harry put his

arm round your waist, and I won't have it.
What's your father thinking about? Why,
that boy's no more fit to be your husband than
that great, ugly, long, brown-bearded Scotchman who poisons the air with his copper-mine,
is to be Louie's."

"Uncle, you are beyond bearing to-day."

"Am I? Well then, be off. But you mind,
Miss Maddy, I won't have it. You'll be silly
enough to marry some day, but when you do,
you shall marry a man, not a feather-headed
young ass, with no more brains than that bass.
Ah, I've got you this time, have I?"

He had thrown in again, and this time
struck and hooked a large fish, whose struggles
he watched with grim satisfaction, till he drew
it gasping and quivering on to the rock—a
fine bass, whose silver sides glistened like
those of a salmon, and whose sharp back
fin stood up ready to cut the unwitting
hand.

"Bad for him, Louie," said the old man
with a laugh; "but one must have dinners,
eh? What a countenance!" he continued,
holding up his fish; "puts me in mind of that
fellow you have up at the house—what's his
name, Priddle, Fiddle?"

"Pràdelle, uncle."

"Ah, Pradelle. Of course he's going back too."

"Yes, uncle."

"Don't like him," continued Uncle Luke, re-baiting quickly and throwing out; "that fellow has got scoundrel written in his face."

"For shame! Mr. Vine," said Madelaine, laughing. "Mr. Pradelle is very gentlemanly and pleasant."

"Good-looking scoundrels always are, my dear. But he don't want you. I watched him. Going to throw over the Scotchman and take to Miss Louie?"

"Uncle, you've got a bite," said the girl coolly.

"Eh? So I have. Got him, too," said the old man, striking and playing his fish just as if he were angling in fresh water. "Thumper."

"What pleasure can it give you to say such unpleasant things, uncle?" continued the girl.

"Truths always are unpleasant," said the old man, laughing. "Don't bother me, there's a shoal off the point now, and I shall get some fish."

"Why, you have all you want now, uncle."

"Rubbish! Shall get a few shillingsworth to sell Mother Perrow."

"Poor Uncle Luke!" said the girl with

mock solemnity; "obliged to fish for his living."

"Better than idling and doing nothing. I like to do it, and—— There he is again. Don't talk."

He hooked and landed another fine bass from the shoal which had come up with the tide that ran like a millstream off the point, when as he placed the fish in the basket he raised his eyes.

"Yah! Go back and look after your men. I thought that would be it. Maddy, look at her cheeks."

"Oh, uncle, if I did not know you to be the best and dearest of——"

"Tchah! Carney!" he cried, screwing up his face. "Look here, I want to catch a few fish and make a little money, so if that long Scot is coming courting, take him somewhere else. Be off!"

"If Mr. Duncan Leslie is coming to say good-day, uncle, I see no reason why he should not say it here," said Louise, calmly enough now, and with the slight flush which had suffused her cheeks fading out.

"Good-day! A great tall sheepish noodle who don't know when he's well off," grumbled the fisher, throwing out once more as a tall gentlemanly-looking young fellow of about eight-and-twenty stepped actively from rock to rock till he had joined the group, raising his soft tweed hat to the ladies and shaking hands.

"What a lovely morning!" he said eagerly. "I saw you come down. Much sport, Mr. Vine?" he added, as he held out his hand.

"No," said Uncle Luke, nodding and holding tightly on to his rod. "Hands full. Can't you see?"

"Oh, yes, I see. One at you now."

"Thankye. Think I couldn't see?" said the old man, striking and missing his fish. "Very kind of you to come and see how I was getting on."

"But I didn't," said the new-comer, smiling. "I knew you didn't want me."

"Here, Louie, make a note of that," said Uncle Luke, sharply. "The Scotch are not so dense as they pretend they are."

"Uncle!"

"Oh, pray don't interpose, Miss Vine. Your uncle and I often have a passage of arms together."

"Well, say what you've got to say, and then go back to your men. Has the vein failed?"

"No, sir; it grows richer every day."

" Sorry for it. I suppose you'll be burrow-
ing under my cottage and burying me one of
these days before my time ? "

" Don't be alarmed, sir."

" I'm not," growled Uncle Luke.

" Uncle is cross, because he is catching more
fish than he wants this morning," said Louise
quietly.

" Hear that, Maddy, my dear ? " said the
old man, sharply. " Here's a problem for
you :—If my niece's tongue is as keen-edged
as that before she is twenty, what will it be at
forty ? "

The girl addressed laughed and shook her
head.

" Any one would think it would be a warn-
ing to any sensible man to keep his distance."

" Uncle ! Pray ! " whispered the niece, looking troubled ; but the old man only chuckled
and hooked another fish.

" Going to make a fortune out of the old
mine, Leslie ? " he said.

" Fortune ? No, sir. A fair income, I
hope."

" Which with prudence and economy—
Scottish prudence and economy—" he added,
meaningly, " would keep you when you got to
be an old man like me. Bah ! "

He snatched out his line and gave an impatient stamp with his foot.

"What is the matter, uncle?"

"What's the matter? It was bad enough before.  Look there!"

# CHAPTER II.

## ELEMENTS OF A WHOLE.

MADELAINE VAN HELDRE had seen the object of Uncle Luke's vexation before he called attention to it; and at the first glance her eyes had lit up with pleasure, but only to give place to an anxious, troubled look, and faint lines came across her brow.

"Why, it is only Harry with his friend," said Louise quietly.

"Yes : flopping and splashing about in the boat. There will not be a fish left when they've done."

"I'll tell them to land at the lower stairs," said Louise eagerly.

"No; let 'em come and do their worst," said the old man, with quite a snarl. "Why doesn't Harry row, instead of letting that miserable cockney fool about with an oar?"

"Miserable cockney!" said Duncan Leslie to himself; and his face, which had been overcast, brightened a little as he scanned the boat coming from the harbour.

"Mr. Pradelle likes exercise," said Louise quietly.

Duncan's face grew dull again.

"Then I wish he would take it in London," said the old man, "jumping over his desk or using his pen, and not come here."

The water glistened and sparkled with the vigorous strokes given by the two young men who propelled the boat, and quickly after there was a grating noise as the bows ground against the rocks of the point and a young man in white flannels leaped ashore, while his companion after awkwardly laying in his oar followed the example, balancing himself as he stepped on to the gunwale, and then, after the fashion of a timid horse at a gutter, making a tremendous bound on to the rocks.

As he did this his companion made a quick leap back into the bows to seize the chain, when he had to put out an oar once more and paddle close up to the rock, the boat having been sent adrift by the force of the other's leap.

"What a fellow you are, Pradelle!" he said, as he jumped on to a rock, and twisted the chain about a block.

" Very sorry, dear boy. Didn't think of that."

" No," said the first sourly, " you didn't."

He was a well-knit manly fellow, singularly like his sister, while his companion, whom he had addressed as Pradelle, seemed to be his very opposite in every way, though on the whole better looking; in fact, his features were remarkably handsome, or would have been had they not been marred by his eyes, which were set close together, and gave him a shifty look.

" How are you, uncle? How do, Leslie?" said Harry, as he stood twirling a gold locket at the end of his chain, to receive a grunt from the fisherman, and a friendly nod from the young mine-owner. " So here you are then," he continued; " we've been looking for you everywhere. You said you were going along the west walk."

" Yes, but we saw uncle fishing, and came down to him."

" Well, come along now."

" Come? Where?"

" Come where? Why for a sail. Wind's just right. Jump in."

Duncan Leslie looked grave, but he brightened a little as he heard what followed.

" Oh, no, Harry."

As she spoke, Louise Vine glanced at her companion, in whose face she read an eager look of acquiescence in the proposed trip, which changed instantly to one of agreement with her negative.

"There, Vic. Told you so. Taken all our trouble for nothing."

"But, Harry——"

"Oh, all right," he cried, interrupting her, in an ill-used tone. "Just like girls. Here's our last day before we go back to the confounded grindstone. We've got the boat, the weather's lovely; we've been looking for you everywhere, and it's 'Oh no, Harry!' And Madelaine looking as if it would be too shocking to go for a sail."

"We don't like to disappoint you," said Madelaine, "but——"

"But you'd rather stay ashore," said the young man shortly. "Never mind, Vic, old chap, we'll go alone, and have a good smoke. Cheerful, isn't it? I say, Uncle Luke, you're quite right."

"First time you ever thought so then," said the old man shortly.

"Perhaps Miss Vine will reconsider her determination," said the young man's companion, in a low soft voice, as he went toward

Louise, and seemed to Duncan Leslie to be throwing all the persuasion possible into his manner.

"Oh no, thank you, Mr. Pradelle," she replied hastily, and Duncan Leslie once more felt relieved and yet pained, for there was a peculiar consciousness in her manner.

"We had brought some cans with us and a hammer and chisel," continued Pradelle. "Harry thought we might go as far as the gorns."

"Zorns, man," cried Harry.

"I beg pardon, zorns, and get a few specimens for Mr. Vine."

"It was very kind and thoughtful of Harry," said Louise hastily, "and we are sorry to disappoint him—on this his last day —but——"

"Blessed *but !*" said Harry, with a sneer ; and he gave Madelaine a withering look, which made her bite her lip.

"And the fish swarming round the point," said Uncle Luke impatiently. "Why don't you go with them, girls ?"

"Right again, uncle," said Harry.

The old man made him a mocking bow.

"Go, uncle ?" said Louise eagerly, and then checking herself.

Duncan Leslie's heart sank like an ingot of his own copper dropped in a tub.

"Yes, go."

"If you think so, uncle——"

"Well, I do," he said testily, "only pray go at once."

"There!" cried Harry. "Come, Maddy."

He held out his hand to his sister's companion, but she hesitated, still looking at Louise, whose colour was going and coming as she saw Pradelle take off his cap and follow his friend's example, holding out his hand to help her into the boat.

"Yes, dear," she said to Madelaine gravely. "They would be terribly disappointed if we did not go."

The next moment Madelaine was in the boat, Louise still hanging back till, feeling that it would be a slight worse than the refusal to go if she ignored the help extended to her, she laid her hand in Pradelle's, and stepped off the rock into the gently rising and falling boat.

"Another of my mistakes," said Duncan Leslie to himself.; and then he started as if some one had given him an electric shock.

"Hullo!" cried the old man. "You're going too?"

"I? going?"

" Yes, of course ! To take care of them. I'm not going to have them set off without some one to act as ballast to those boys."

Louise mentally cast her arms round the old man's neck and kissed him.

Harry, in the same manner, kicked his uncle into the sea, and Pradelle's eyes looked closer together than usual, as he turned them upon the young mine-owner.

" I should only be too happy," said the latter, " if——"

" Oh, there's plenty of room, Mr. Leslie," cried the girls in duet. " Pray come."

The invitation was so genuine that Leslie's heart seemed to leap.

" Oh yes, plenty of room," said Harry, " only if the wind drops, you'll have to pull an oar."

" Of course," said Leslie, stepping in.

Harry raised the boat-hook, and thrust the little vessel away, and then began to step the mast.

" Lay hold of the rudder, Leslie," he cried. " Send us up some fish for tea, uncle."

" I'll wait and see first whether you come back," said the old man. " Good-bye, girls. Don't be uneasy. I'll go and tell the old people if you're drowned."

"Thank you," shouted back the young man
as he hoisted the little sail, which began to fill
at once, and by the time he had it sheeted
home, the boat was swiftly running eastward
with the water pattering against her bows, and
a panorama of surpassing beauty seeming to
glide slowly by them on the left.

"There!" cried Harry to his friend, who
had seated himself rather sulkily forward, the
order to take the tiller having placed Leslie
between Louise and Madelaine. "Make much
of it, Vic: Paddington to-morrow night, han-
som cab or the Underground, and next morning
the office. Don't you feel happy?"

"Yes, now," said Pradelle, with a glance at
Louise.

"Easy, Leslie, easy," cried Harry; "where
are you going?"

"I beg pardon," said the young man hastily,
for he had unwittingly changed the course of
the boat.

"That's better. Any one would think you
wanted to give Uncle Luke the job he talked
about."

Madelaine looked up hastily.

"No; we will not do that, Miss Van Heldre," said Leslie smiling. "Shall I hold the
sheet, Vine?"

"No need," said the young man, making the rope fast.

"But——"

"Oh, all right. I know what you're going to say—puff of wind might lay us over as we pass one of the combes. Wasn't born here for nothing."

Leslie said no more, but deferred to the opinion of the captain of the boat.

"Might as well have brought a line to trail. You'd have liked to fish, wouldn't you, Vic?"

"Only when we are alone," said Pradelle. "Can you tell me the name of that point, Miss Vine?"

"Brea," said Louise quietly.

"And that little valley?"

"Tol Du. The old Cornish names must sound strange to any one from London."

"Oh no," he said, bending forward to engage her in conversation. "This place is very interesting, and I shall regret going," he added with a sigh, and a thoughtful look toward the picturesque little group of houses on either side of the estuary.

"I should think you will," said Harry. "Never mind, we've had a very jolly time. I say, Maddy," he whispered, "you will write to a fellow, won't you?"

"No," she said quietly; "there is no need."

"No need?"

"Louie will be writing to you every week, and you will answer her. I shall hear how you are getting on."

Harry whistled and looked angrily at his sister, who was replying to some remark made by Leslie.

"Here, Vic," he said, "she's too heavy forward. Come and sit by my sister. That's better. A little more over to the side, Leslie. Always trim your boat."

The changes were made, and the little yawl sped rapidly on past the headland of gray granite hoary and shaggy with moss; past black frowning masses of slaty shale, over and amongst which the waves broke in sparkling foam, and on and on by ferny hollows and rifts, down which trickled tiny streams. The day was glorious, and the reflection of the sapphire sky dyed the sea tint of a blue that seemed amethystine in its richer transparent hue. The gray gulls floated overhead, and the tiny fish they pursued made the sea flash as they played about and showed their silvery sides.

But the conversation flagged. Possibly the

fact of its being the last day of a pleasant sojourn acted upon the spirits of two of the party, while the third of the male occupants of the boat rather welcomed the restraint and silence, for it gave him an opportunity to sit and think and wonder what was to be his future, and what the animated countenance of Louise Vine meant as she answered the questions of her brother's friend.

He was a visitor as well as her brother's companion ; he had been staying at Mr. Vine's for a fortnight. They had had endless opportunities for conversation, and—in short, Duncan Leslie felt uncomfortable.

It was then with a feeling of relief that was shared by both the ladies, that after a few miles run Henry Vine stood up in the bows, and, keeping a sharp look out for certain rocks, shouted his orders to Leslie as to the steering of the boat, and finally, as they neared the frowning cliffs, suddenly lowered the sail and took up the oars.

They were abreast of a large cave, where the swift gray-winged pigeons flew in and out over the swelling waves, which seemed to glide slowly on and on, to rush rapidly after the birds and disappear in the gloom beneath the arch. Then there was a low echoing boom as the wave struck far away in the cave, and came back hissing and whispering to be merged in the next.

"Going to row close in?" said Leslie, scanning the weird, forbidding place rather anxiously.

"Going to row right in," said Harry, with a contemptuous smile. "Not afraid, are you?"

"Can't say," replied Leslie. "A little perhaps. The place does not look tempting. Do you think it is safe to go in?"

"Like to land on the rock till we come back?" said Harry, instead of answering the question.

"No," said Leslie quietly; "but do you think it wise to row in there?"

"You're not afraid, are you, girls?"

"I always feel nervous till we are outside again," said Louise quietly.

"But you will be very careful, Harry," said Madelaine.

"Think I want to drown myself?" he said bitterly. "I might just as well, p'r'aps, as go back to that dismal office in London, to slave from morning till night."

He rested upon his oars for a minute or two, and perhaps from the reflection of the masses of ferns which fringed the arch of the cavern, and which were repeated in the clear waters, Victor Pradelle's face seemed to turn of a sickly green, while one hand grasped the edge of the boat with spasmodic force.

"Now then, hold tight," said the rower, as a swell came from seaward, running right in and raising the boat so that by skilful management she was borne forward right beneath the arch and then away into the depths of the cavern, leaving her rocking upon the watery floor, while it sped on away into the darkness, where it broke with a booming noise which echoed, and whispered, and died away in sobs, and sighs, and strange hisses and gasps, as if the creatures which made the cavern their lair had been disturbed, and were settling down again to sleep.

"There, Vic," cried Harry, "what do you think of this?"

Pradelle was holding tightly by the side of the boat, and gazing uneasily round.

"Think? Yes: very wild and wonderful," he said huskily.

"Wonderful? I should think it is. Goes in ever so far, only it isn't wide enough for the boat."

Leslie looked back at the mouth, fringed with the fronds of ferns, and at the lovely picture it framed of sunny amethystine sea; then at the rocky sides, dripping with moisture, and here of a rich metallic green, there covered with glistening weeds of various shades of olive-green and brown.

"Ahoy—oy!" shouted Harry with all his might, and at the same moment he let his oars splash in the water.

Pradelle leaped to his feet as there came a strange echo and a whirring rush, and a dozen pigeons swept past their heads from out of the depths of the water cave, and away into the brilliant sunshine.

"Oh, if I had a gun," cried Pradelle, to hide his confusion.

"What for—to make a miss?" sneered Harry. "Now then, out with those cans. Fill every one, and I'll try and knock off a few anemones for the governor."

As he spoke he laid in his oars, picked a hammer and chisel from out of the locker in the forepart of the boat, and then worked it along by the side of the great cave, as from out of the clefts and crannies above and beneath the water he searched for the semi-gelatinous sea-anemones that clustered among barnacles, and the snail-like whorl molluscs whose home was on the weedy rocks.

The girls aided all they could, pointing out and receiving in the tins a many-rayed creature, which closed up till it resembled a gout of blood; now still adhering to the rock which Harry chipped off, a beautiful *Actinia* of olive-green with gem-like spots around the mouth and amid its fringe, of turquoise blue.

Duncan Leslie eagerly lent his help; and, not to be behindhand, Pradelle took up the boat-hook and held on, but with the smoothness and care of a sleek tom-cat, he carefully avoided wetting his hands.

"Nothing very new here," said Harry at last, as the waves that kept coming in made the boat rise and fall gently; "there's another better cave than this close by. Let's go there; or what do you say to stopping here and having a smoke till the tide has risen and shut us in?"

"Is there any risk of that?" said Pradelle anxiously.

"Oh, yes, plenty."

Leslie glanced at Louisa and thought that it would be very pleasant to play protector all through the darkness till the way was open and daylight shone again. He caught her

eyes more than once and tried to read them
as he wondered whether there was hope for
him ; but so surely as she found him gazing
rather wistfully at her, she hurriedly continued
the collecting, pointing out one of the beautiful objects they sought beneath the surface,
and asking Pradelle to shift the boat a little
farther along.

"All my vanity and conceit," said Leslie
to himself with a sigh ; "and why should I
worry myself about a woman ?  I have plenty
to do without thinking of love and marriage.
If I did, why not begin to dream about
pleasant, straightforward Madelaine Van
Heldre ?  There can be nothing more than
a friendly feeling towards Master Harry
here."

"Now then, sit fast," cried the latter object
of his thoughts ; "and if we are capsized,
girls, I'll look after you, Maddy.  Pradelle
here will swim out with Louie, and I shall
leave you to bring out the boat, Leslie.  You
can swim, can't you ?"

"A little," said the young man dryly.

Pradelle looked rather more green, for the
light within the cave was of a peculiar hue,
and he began to think uneasily of bathing
out of a machine at Margate, holding on to

a rope, and also of the effort he once made to swim across a tepid bath in town. But he laughed heartily directly after as he realized that it was all banter on his friend's part, while, in spite of himself, he gave a sigh of relief as, riding out on the crest of a broken wave, they once more floated in the sunshine.

Ten minutes' careful rowing among the rocks, which were now four or five feet beneath the water, now showing their weedy crests above, brought them to the mouth of another cave, only approachable from the sea, and sending the boat in here, the collection went on till it was deemed useless to take more specimens, when they passed out again, greatly to Pradelle's satisfaction.

"How's time?" said Harry. "Half-past four? Plenty of time. High tea at six. What shall we do—sail right out and tack, or row along here in the smooth water among the rocks?"

"Row slowly back," said Louise; and Pradelle took an oar.

At the end of half a mile he ceased rowing.

"Tired?" said Harry.

"No; I have a blister on my hand; that's all."

"Come and pull, Leslie," said Harry. "You'd better steer, Louie, and don't send us on to a rock."

The exchange of places was made, and once more they began to progress with the boat, travelling far more swiftly as they glided on close in to the mighty cliff which rose up overhead, dappled with mossy gray and patches of verdure, dotted with yellow and purple blooms.

"To go on like this for ever!" thought Leslie as he swung to and fro, his strong muscles making the water foam as he dipped his oar, watching Louise as she steered, and seemed troubled and ready to converse with Pradelle whenever she caught his eye.

"Starn all!" shouted Harry suddenly, as about three miles from home they came abreast of a narrow opening close to the surface of the water.

The way of the boat was checked, and Harry looked at the hole into which the tide ran and ebbed as the swell rose and fell, now nearly covering the opening, now leaving it three or four feet wide.

"Bound to say there are plenty of good specimens in there," he said. "What do you say, Vic, shall we go in?"

" Impossible."

" Not it. Bound to say that's the opening to quite a large zorn. I've seen the seals go in there often."

" Has it ever been explored ? " said Leslie, who felt interested in the place.

" No ; it's nearly always covered. It's only at low tides like this that the opening is bared. If the girls were not here I'd go in."

" How ? " said Pradelle.

" How ?—why swim in."

" And be shut up by the tide and drowned," said Louise.

" Good thing too," said Harry, with the same look of a spoiled boy at Madelaine. " I don't find life go very jolly. Boat wouldn't pass in there."

He had risen from his seat and was standing with one foot on the gunwale, the other on the thwart, gazing curiously at the dark orifice some forty yards away, the boat rising and falling as it swayed here and there on the waves, which ran up to the face of the cliff and back, when just as the attention of all was fixed upon the little opening, from which came curious hissing and rushing noises, the boat rose on a good-sized swell, and as it sank was left upon the top of a weedy rock which seemed to rise like the shaggy head of a huge sea monster beneath the keel.

There was a bump, a grinding, grating noise, a shout and a heavy splash, and the boat, after narrowly escaping being capsized, floated once more in deep water; but Harry had lost his balance, gone overboard, and disappeared.

Madelaine uttered a cry of horror, and then for a few moments there was a dead silence, during which Louise sat with blanched face, parted lips, and dilated eyes, gazing at the spot where her brother had disappeared. Pradelle held on by the side of the boat, and Leslie sprang up, rapidly stripped off coat and vest, and stood ready to plunge in.

Those moments seemed indefinitely prolonged, and a terrible feeling of despair began to attack the occupants of the boat as thought after thought, each of the blackest type, flashed through their brains. He had been sucked down by the undertow, and was being carried out to sea—he was entangled in the slimy sea wrack, and could not rise again—he had struck his head against the rocks, stunned himself, and gone down like a stone, and so on.

Duncan Leslie darted one glance at the pale and suffering face of the sister, placed a foot on the gunwale, and was in the act of gathering himself up to spring from the boat, when Harry's head rose thirty yards away.

"Ahoy!" he shouted, as he began to paddle and tread water. "Hallo, Leslie, ready for a bathe? Come out! Water's beautiful. Swim you back to the harbour."

There was a long-drawn breath in the boat which sounded like a groan, as the terrible mental pressure was removed, and the young man began to swim easily and slowly towards his friends.

"Mind she doesn't get on another rock, Leslie," he cried.

"Here, catch hold of this," cried Pradelle, whose face was ashy, and he held out the boat-hook as far as he could reach.

"Thank ye," said Harry mockingly, and twenty yards away. "Little farther, please. What a lovely day for a swim!"

"Harry, pray come into the boat," cried Louise excitedly.

"What for? Mind the porpoise."

He gave a few sharp blows on the water with his hands, raising himself up and turning right over, dived, his legs just appearing above the surface, and then there was an eddy where he had gone down.

" Don't be frightened," whispered Madelaine, whose voice sounded a little husky.

" Here we are again ! " cried Harry, reappearing close to the boat and spluttering the water from his lips, as with all the gaiety of a boy he looked mirthfully at the occupants of the boat. " Any orders for pearls, ladies ? "

" Don't be foolish, Harry," cried Louise, as he swam close to them.

" Not going to be. I say, Leslie, take the boat-hook away from that fellow, or he'll be making a hole in the bottom of the boat."

As he spoke, he laid a hand upon the gunwale and looked merrily from one to the other.

" Don't touch me, girls. I'm rather damp," he said. " I say, what a capital bathing dress flannels make ! "

" Shall I help you in ? " said Leslie.

" No, thank ye, I'm all right. As I am in, I may as well have a swim."

" No, no, Harry, don't be foolish," cried Louise.

" There, you'd better hitch a rope round me, and tow me behind, or I shall swamp the boat."

" Harry ! what are you going to do ? " cried

Madelaine, as he loosed his hold of the gun-wale, and began to swim away.

"Wait a bit and you'll see," he cried. "Leslie, you take care of the boat. I shan't be long."

"But, Harry——"

"All right, I tell you."

"Where are you going?"

"In here," he shouted back, and he swam straight to the low opening at the foot of the massive granite cliff, paddled a little at the mouth till the efflux of water was over, and then as a fresh wave came, he took a few strokes, gave a shout, and to the horror of the two girls seemed to be sucked right into the opening.

As he disappeared, he gave another shout, a hollow strange echoing "Good-bye," and a few moments after there was a run back of the water and a hollow roar, and it needed very little exercise of the imagination to picture the rugged opening as the mouth of some marine monster into which the young man had passed.

# CHAPTER III.

## DISCORDS.

"Don't be alarmed," said Leslie quietly; "I dare say it is like one of the zorns yonder, only the mouth is too narrow for a boat."

"But it is so foolish," said Louise, giving him a grateful look.

"Yes, but he swims so easily and well, there is nothing to mind. What are you going to do, Mr. Pradelle?"

"Work the boat close up so as to help him," said Pradelle shortly.

"No, don't do that. We have had one escape from a capsize. We must keep out here in deep water."

Pradelle frowned.

"I think I know what I'm about, sir," he said sharply; "do you suppose I am going to sit here when my friend may be in danger?"

"I have no doubt you know what you are about in London, sir," said Leslie quietly, "but this is not a pavement in the Strand, and it is not safe to take the boat closer in."

Pradelle was about to make some retort, but Louise interposed.

"Try if you can get nearer the mouth of that dreadful place, Mr. Leslie," she said, "I am getting terribly alarmed."

Leslie seated himself, took the oars, turned the boat, and backed slowly and cautiously in, holding himself ready to pull out again at the slightest appearance of danger. For the sea rushed against the rocky barrier with tremendous force, while even on this calm day the swing and wash and eddy amongst the loose rocks was formidable.

By skilful management Leslie backed the boat to within some thirty feet of the opening; but the position was so perilous that he had to pull out for a few yards to avoid a couple of rocks, which in the movement of the clear water seemed to be rising toward them from time to time, and coming perilously near.

Then he shouted, but there was no answer. He shouted again and again, but there was no reply, and a chill of horror, intensifying from moment to moment, came upon all.

"Harry! Harry!" cried Louise, now raising

her voice, as Madelaine crept closer to her and
clutched her hand.

But there was no reply. No sound but the
rush and splash and hiss of the waters as they
struck the rocks, and came back broken from
the attack.

"What folly!" muttered Leslie, with his
face growing rugged. Then quickly, "I don't
think you need feel alarmed ; I dare say he
has swum in for some distance, and our voices
do not reach him. Stop a moment."

He suddenly remembered a little gold dog-
whistle at his watch-chain, and raising it to
his lips he blew long and shrilly, till the ear-
piercing note echoed along the cliff, and the
gulls came floating lazily overhead and peering
wonderingly down.

"I say, Harry, old man, come out now,"
cried Pradelle, and then rising from his seat,
he placed his hands on either side of his lips,
and uttered the best imitation he could manage
of the Australian call, "Coo-ey ! Coo-ey !"

There were echoes and whispers, and the
rush and hiss of the water. Then two or three
times over there came from out of the opening
a peculiar dull hollow sound, such as might
be made by some great animal wallowing far
within.

"Mr. Leslie," said Louise, in a low appealing voice, "what shall we do?"

"Oh, wait a few minutes, my dear Miss Vine," interposed Pradelle, hastily. "He'll be out directly. I assure you there is no cause for alarm."

Leslie frowned, but his face coloured directly, for his heart gave a great throb.

Louise paid not the slightest heed to Pradelle's words, and kept her limpid eyes fixed appealingly upon Leslie's, as if she looked to him for help.

"I hardly know what to do," he said in a low business-like tone. "I dare not leave you without some one to manage the boat, or I would go in."

"Yes, yes, pray go!" she said excitedly. "Never mind us."

"We could each take an oar and keep the boat here," said Madelaine quickly; "we can both row."

"No, really; I'll manage the boat," said Pradelle.

"I think you had better leave it to the ladies, Mr. Pradelle," said Leslie coldly. "They know the coast."

"Well really, sir, I——"

"This is no time for interference," cried

Madelaine, with a flush of excitement, and she caught hold of an oar. " Louie dear, quick!"

The other oar was resigned, and as Leslie passed aft, he gave Louise one quick look, reading in her face, as he believed, trust and thankfulness and then dread.

"No, no, Mr. Leslie, I hardly dare let you go," she faltered.

*Plash!*

The boat was rolling and dancing on the surface, relieved of another burden, and Duncan Leslie was swimming toward the opening.

The two girls dipped their oars from time to time, for their sea-side life had given them plenty of experience of the management of a boat; and as Pradelle sat looking sulky and ill-used, they watched the swimmer as he too timed his movements, so that he gradually approached, and then in turn was sucked right into the weird water-way, which might lead another into some terrible chasm from which there was no return.

A low hoarse sigh, as if one had whispered while suffering pain the word " Hah!" and then with dilated eyes the two girls sat watching the black opening for what seemed a terrible interval of time, before, to their intense relief, there came a shout of laughter, followed by the appearance of Leslie, who swam out looking stern, and closely followed by Harry.

"It is not the sort of fun I can appreciate, Miss Vine," said Leslie, turning as he reached the stern of the boat.

"Well, I know that," cried Harry mockingly. "Scotchmen never can appreciate a joke."

"There, ladies, what did I tell you?" cried Pradelle triumphantly.

There was no reply, and the visitor from London winced, for his presence in the boat seemed to be thoroughly *de trop*.

"Miss Vine—Miss Van Heldre," said Leslie quietly, "will you change places now? Get right aft, and we will climb in over the bows."

"But the boat?" faltered Louise, whose emotion was so great that she could hardly trust herself to speak.

"We'll see to that," said Leslie. "Your brother and I will row back."

It did not seem to trouble him now that the two girls took their places, one on either side of Pradelle, while as soon as they were seated he climbed in streaming with water, seating himself on the gunwale, Harry climbing in on the other side.

"Harry, how could you?" cried Louise, now, with an indignant look.

"Easily enough," he said, seating himself calmly. "Thought you'd lost me?"

He looked at Madelaine as he spoke, but she turned her face away, biting her lips, and it was Louise who replied,

"I did not think you could have been so cruel."

"Cruel be hanged!" he retorted. "Thought I'd find out whether I was of any consequence after all. You people seem to say I'm of none. Did they begin to cry, Vic?"

"Oh, I'm not going to tell tales," said Pradelle with a smile.

"I should have had a pipe in there, only my matches had got wet."

"Ha-ha-ha!" laughed Pradelle, and the mirth sounded strange there beneath the rocks, and a very decided hiss seemed to come from out of the low rugged opening.

"Try again, Vic," said Harry mockingly; but his friend made no reply, for he was staring hard and defiantly at Leslie, who, as he handled his oar, gave him a calmly contemptuous look that galled him to the quick.

" Ready, Leslie ? " said Harry.

" Yes."

The oars dipped, Leslie pulling stroke, and the boat shot out from its dangerous position among the rocks, rose at a good-sized swelling wave, topped it, seemed to hang as in a balance for a moment, and then glided down and went forward in response to a few vigorous strokes.

"Never mind the tiller, Vic," said Harry; " let it swing. We can manage without that. All right, girls ? "

There was no reply.

"Sulky, eh ? Well, I'd a good mind to stop in. Sorry you got so wet, Leslie."

Still no reply.

" Cheerful party, 'pon my word ! " said Harry with a contemptuous laugh. "Hope no one objects to my smoking."

He looked hard at Madelaine, but she avoided his gaze, and he uttered a short laugh.

"Got a cigar to spare, Vic ? "

" Yes, dear boy, certainly."

" Pass it along then, and the lights. Hold hard a minute, Leslie."

The latter ceased rowing as Pradelle handed a cigar and the matches to his friend.

"Will you take one, Mr. Leslie?" said Pradelle.

"Thanks, no," said Leslie quietly, and to the would-be donor's great relief, for he had only two left. Then once more the rowing was resumed, Pradelle striking a match to light a cigar for himself, and then recollecting himself and throwing the match away.

"Well, we're enjoying ourselves!" cried Harry after they had proceeded some distance in silence. "I say, Vic, say something!"

Pradelle had been cudgelling his brains for the past ten minutes, but the more he tried to find something *à propos* the more every pleasant subject seemed to recede.

In fact it would have been difficult just then for the most accomplished talker to have set all present at their ease, for Harry's folly had moved his sister so that she feared to speak lest she should burst into a hysterical fit of weeping, and Madelaine, as she sat there with her lips compressed, felt imbued with but one desire, which took the form of the following words :

"Oh, how I should like to box his ears!"

"Getting dry, Leslie?" said Harry after a long silence.

"Not very," was the reply.

" Ah, well, there's no fear of our catching cold pulling like this."

" Not the slightest," said Leslie coldly ; then there was another period of silence, during which the water seemed to patter and slap the bows of the boat, while the panorama of rock and foam and glittering cascade, as the crags were bathed by the Atlantic swell, and it fell back broken, seemed perfectly fresh and new as seen from another point of view.

At last Harry, after trying two or three times more to start a conversation, said shortly—

" Well, this is my last day at home, and I think I ought to say, ' Thank goodness ! ' This is coming out for a pleasant sail, and having to row back like a galley-slave ! Oh, I beg your pardon, ladies ! All my mistake. I am highly complimented. All this glumminess is because I am going away."

He received such a look of reproach that he uttered an angry ejaculation and began to pull so hard that Leslie had to second his movement to keep the boat's head straight for the harbour, whose farther point soon after came in sight, with two figures on the rocks at the end.

"Papa along with Uncle Luke," said Louise softly.

"Eh?" said Harry sharply; "the old man still fishing?"

"Yes," said Louise rather coldly; "and, Maddy, dear, is not that Mr. Van Heldre?"

Madelaine shaded her eyes from the western sun, where it was sinking fast, and nodded.

"Where shall we land you?" said Harry sulkily now, "at the point, or will you go up the harbour?"

"If there is not too much sea on, at the point," said Louise gravely.

"Oh, I dare say we can manage that without wetting your plumes," said the young man contemptuously; and after another ten minutes' pulling they reached the harbour mouth and made for the point, where Uncle Luke stood leaning on his rod watching the coming boat, in company with a tall gray man with refined features, who had taken off the straw hat he wore to let the breeze play through his closely cut hair, while from time to time he turned to speak either to Uncle Luke or to the short thick-set man who, with his pointed white moustache and closely clipped peaked beard, looked in his loose holland blouse like a French officer taking his vacation at the sea-side.

"Mind how you come," said the latter in a sharp, decided way. "Watch your time, Leslie. Back in, my lad. Can you manage it, girls?"

"Oh, yes," they cried confidently.

"Sit still then till the boat's close in, then one at a time. You first, my dear."

This to Louise, as he stepped actively down the granite rocks to a narrow natural shelf, which was now bare, now several inches deep in water.

"If we manage it cleverly we can get you ashore without a wetting."

The warnings were necessary, for the tide ran fast, and the Atlantic swell made the boat rise and fall, smooth as the surface was.

"Now then," cried the French-looking gentleman, giving his orders as if he were an officer in command, "easy, Harry Vine; back a little, Mr. Leslie. Be ready, Louie, my dear. That's it; a little more. I have you. Bravo!"

The words came slowly, and with the latter there was a little action; as he took the hands outstretched to him, when the boat nearly grazed the rock, there was a light spring, the girl was on the narrow shelf, and the boat, in answer to a touch of the oars, was half a dozen yards away, rising and falling on the swell.

"Give me your hand, my dear," said the tall gray gentleman, leaning down.

"Oh, I can manage, papa," she cried, and the next moment she was by his side. Looking back, "Thank you, Mr. Van Heldre," she said.

"Eh? All right, my child. Now, Maddy. Steady, my lads. Mind that ledge; don't get her under there. Bravo! that's right. Now, my girl. Well done!"

Madelaine leaped to his side, and was in turn assisted to the top, she accepting the tall gentleman's help, while Uncle Luke, with his hands resting on his rod, which he held with the butt on the rock, stood grimly looking down at the boat.

"I think I'll land here," said Leslie. "You don't want my help with the boat."

"Oh, no; we can manage," said Harry sourly; and Leslie gave up his oar and leaped on to the rock as the boat was again backed in.

"That chap looks quite green," said Uncle Luke with a sneering laugh. "Our London friend been poorly, Louie?"

Before she could answer the tall gentleman cried to those in the boat—

"Don't be long, my boy. Tea will be waiting."

"All right, dad. Lay hold of this oar, Vic, and let's get her moored."

"Why, you're wet, Mr. Leslie," said the tall gentleman, shaking hands.

"Only sea-water, sir. It's nothing."

"But," said the former speaker, looking quickly from one to the other, and his handsome, thoughtful face seemed troubled, "has there been anything wrong?"

"Harry fell in," said Louise, speaking rather quickly and excitedly; "and Mr. Leslie——"

"Ah!" ejaculated the tall gentleman excitedly.

"It was nothing, sir," said Leslie hastily. "He swam in among the rocks—into a cave, and he was a long time gone, and I went after him; that's all."

"But, my dear boy, you must make haste and change your things."

"I shall not hurt, Mr. Vine."

"And—and—look here. Make haste and come on then to us. There will be a meal ready. It's Harry's last day at home."

"Oh, thank you, Mr. Vine; I don't think I'll come to-night."

"But you have been one of the party so far, and I should—Louie, my dear——"

"We shall be very glad if you will come, Mr. Leslie," said Louise, in response to her father's hesitating words and look, and there was a calm, ingenuous invitation in her words that made the young man's heart throb.

"I, too, shall be very glad," he said quietly.

"That's right, that's right," said Mr. Vine, laying one of his long thin white hands on the young man's arm; and then changing its position, so that he could take hold of one of the buttons on his breast. Then turning quickly: "Madelaine's coming, of course."

"Louie says so," said the girl quietly.

"To be sure; that's right, my dear; that's right," said the old man, beaming upon her as he took one of her hands to hold and pat it in his. "You'll come too, Van?"

"I? No, no. I've some bills of lading to look over."

"Yah!" ejaculated Uncle Luke with a snarl.

"Yes; bills of lading, you idle old cynic. I can't spend my time fishing."

"Pity you can't," said Uncle Luke. "Money, money, always money."

"Hear him, Mr. Leslie?" said Van Heldre smiling. "Are you disposed to follow his teachings?"

"I'm afraid not," said Leslie.

"Not he," snarled Uncle Luke.

"But you will come, Van?" said Mr. Vine.

"My dear fellow, I wish you would not tempt me. There's work to do. Then there's my wife."

"Bring Mrs. Van Heldre too," said Louise, laying her hand on his.

"Ah, you temptress," he cried merrily.

"It's Harry's last evening," said Mr. Vine.

"Look here," said Van Heldre, "will you sing me my old favourite if I come, Louie?"

"Yes; and you shall have a duet too."

"Ah, never mind the duet," said Van Heldre laughingly; "I can always hear Maddy at home. There, out of pocket again by listening to temptation. I'll come."

"Come and join us too, Luke," said Mr. Vine.

"No!" snapped the old fisher.

"Do, uncle," said Louise.

"Shan't," he snarled, stooping to pick up his heavy basket.

" But it's Harry's last——"

" Good job too," snarled the old man.

" I'm going your way, Mr. Luke Vine," said Leslie. " Let me carry the basket."

" Thank ye; I'm not above carrying my own fish," said the old man sharply; and he raised and gave the basket a swing to get it upon his back, but tottered with the weight, and nearly fell on the uneven rocks.

" There, it is too heavy for you," said Leslie, taking possession of the basket firmly; and Louise Vine's eyes brightened.

" Be too heavy for you when you get as old as I am," snarled the old man.

" I dare say," said Leslie quietly; and they went off together.

" Luke's in fine form this afternoon," said Van Heldre, nodding and smiling.

" Yes," said the brother, looking after him wistfully. " We shall wait till you come, Mr. Leslie," he shouted, giving vent to an after-thought.

The young man turned and waved his hand.

" Rather like Leslie," said Van Heldre. " Maddy, you'll have to set your cap at him."

Madelaine looked up at him and laughed.

"Yes, poor Luke!" said Mr. Vine thoughtfully, as he stooped and picked up a small net and a tin can, containing the treasures he had found in sundry rock pools. "I'm afraid we are a very strange family, Van," he added, as they walked back towards the little town.

"Very, old fellow," said his friend, smiling. "I'll be with you before Leslie gets back, wife and the necessary change of dress permitting."

# CHAPTER IV.

## A THUNDERBOLT.

GEORGE VINE, gentleman, as he was set down in the parish books and the West-country directory, lived in a handsome old granite-built residence that he had taken years before, when, in obedience to his sister's wish, he had retired from the silk trade a wealthy man. But there he had joined issue with the lady in question, obstinately refusing to make France his home, and selecting the house above named in the old Cornish port for two reasons : one, to be near his old friend Godfrey Van Heldre, a well-to-do merchant who carried on rather a mixed business, dealing largely in pilchards, which he sent in his own ships to the Italian ports, trading in return in such produce of the Levant as oranges, olives, and dried fruit; the other, so that he could devote himself to the branch of natural history, upon which he had grown to be an authority so great that his work upon the Actiniadæ of our coast was looked forward to with no little expectation by a good many people, in addition to those who wrote F.Z.S. at the end of their names.

The pleasant social meal known as high tea was spread in the long low oak-panelled dining-room, whose very wide bay window looked right over the town from its shelf upon the huge granite cliffs, and far away westward from whence came the gales which beat upon the old mansion, whose granite sides and gables had turned them off for the past two hundred years.

It was a handsomely furnished room, thoroughly English, and yet with a suggestion of French in the paintings of courtly-looking folk, which decorated the panels above the old oak sideboard and dressers, upon which stood handsome old chased cups, flagons and salvers battered and scratched, but rich and glistening old silver all the same, and looking as if the dents and scratches were only the natural puckers and furrows such venerable pieces of plate should possess.

There was another suggestion of the foreign element, too, in the glazing of the deeply embayed window, for right across and between

all the mullions, the leaden lattice panes gave
place, about two-thirds of the way up, to a
series of artistically painted armorial bearings
in stained glass, shields and helmets with
their crests and supporters, and beneath the
scutcheon in the middle, a ribbon with triple
curve and fold bearing the words *Roy et Foy*.

The furniture had been selected to be
thoroughly in keeping with the antiquity of
the mansion, and the old oak chairs and so
much of the table as could be seen for the
long fine white linen cloth was of the oldest
and darkest oak.

The table was spread with the abundant
fare dear to West-country folk; fruit and
flowers gave colour, and the thick yellow
cream and white sugar were piled high in
silver bowls. The great tea urn was hissing
upon its stand, the visitors had arrived, and
the host was dividing his time between fidget-
ing to and fro from the door to Van Heldre,
who was leaning up against one of the mullions
of the great bay window talking to Leslie upon
subjects paramount in Cornwall—fish and the
yielding of the mines.

The young people were standing about
talking, Louise with her hand resting on the
chair where sat a pleasant-looking, rosy little

woman with abundant white hair, and her
mittened hands crossed over the waist of her
purple velvet gown enriched with good French
lace.

"Margaret Vine's keeping us waiting a long
time this evening," she said.

"Mamma!" said Madelaine reproachfully.

"Well, my dear, it's the simple truth.
And so you go back to business to-morrow,
Harry?"

"Yes, Mrs. Van Heldre. Slave again."

"Nonsense, my boy. Work's good for
every one. I'm sure your friend, Mr. Pradelle,
thinks so," she continued, appealing to that
gentleman.

"Well," he said, with an unpleasant laugh,
"nobody left me a fortune, so I'm obliged to
say yes."

"Ah, here she is!" said Mr. Vine, with a
sigh of relief, as the door opened, and with
almost theatrical effect a rather little sharp-
looking woman of about sixty entered, gazing
quickly round and pausing just within the
room to make an extremely formal old-fashioned
courtesy—sinking nearly to the ground as if
she were a telescopic figure disappearing into
the folds of the stiff rich brocade silk dress, of
a wonderful pattern of pink and green, and

cut in a fashion probably popular at Versailles
a hundred years ago.    She did not wear
powder, but her white hair turned up and
piled upon her head after the fashion of that
blooming period, produced the same effect;
and as she gave the fan she held a twitch
which spread it open with a loud rattling
noise, she seemed, with her haughty carriage,
handsome aquiline face with long chin, that
appeared to have formed the pattern for her
stomacher, like one of the paintings on the
panelled wall suddenly come to life, and feeling strange at finding herself among that
modern company.

"I hope you have not waited for me," she
said, smiling and speaking in a high-pitched
musical voice.    "Louise, my child, you should
not.    Ah!" she continued, raising her gold-
rimmed eye-glass to her thin arched nose and
dropping it directly, "Mrs. Van Heldre, Mr.
Van Heldre, pray be seated.    Mr. Victor
Pradelle, will you be so good?"

The young man had gone through the per-
formance several times before, and he was in
waiting ready to take the tips of the gloved
fingers extended to him, and walking over the
thick Turkey carpet with the lady to the
other end of the room in a way that seemed

to endow him with a court suit and a sword, and suggested the probability of the couple continuing their deportment walk to the polished oak boards beyond the carpet, and then after sundry bows and courtesies going through the steps of the *minuet de la cour.*

As a matter of fact, Pradelle led the old girl, as he called her, to the seat she occupied at the end of the table, when she condescended to leave her room; the rest of the company took their seats, and the meal began.

Harry had tried to ensconce himself beside Madelaine, but that young lady had made a sign to Duncan Leslie, who eagerly took the chair beside her, one which he coveted, for it was between her and Louise, now busy with the tea-tray; and in a sulky manner, Harry obeyed the motion of the elderly lady's fan.

"That's right, Henri, *mon cher,*" she said, smiling, "come and sit by me. I shall miss you so, my darling, when you are gone back to that horrible London, and that wretched business."

"Don't, don't, don't, Margaret, my dear," said Mr. Vine, good-humouredly. "You will make him unhappy at having to leave home."

"I hope so, George," said the lady with dignity, and pronouncing his Christian name

with the softness peculiar to the French
tongue; "and," she added with a smile,
"especially as we have company, will you
oblige me—Marguerite, if you please?"

"Certainly, certainly, my dear."

"Is that Miss Van Heldre?" said the lady,
raising her glass once more. "I beg your
pardon, my child; I hope you are well."

"Quite well, thank you, Miss Marguerite
Vine," said Madelaine quietly, and her bright
young face looked perfectly calm, though there
was a touch of sarcasm in her tone.

"Louise, dearest, my tea a little sweeter,
please."

The meal progressed, and the stiffness produced by the *entrée* of the host's sister—it
was her own term for her appearance—soon
wore off, the lady being very quiet as she
discussed the viands placed before her with
a very excellent appetite. Mrs. Van Heldre
prattled pleasantly on, with plenty of homely
common-sense, to her host. Van Heldre threw
in a word now and then, joked Louise and his
daughter, and made a wrinkle on his broad
forehead, which was his way of making a note.

The note he made was that a suspicion
which had previously entered his brain was
correct.

"He's taken with her," he said to himself, as he glanced at Louise and then at Duncan Leslie, who seemed to be living in a dream. As a rule he was an energetic, quick, and sensible man; on this occasion he was particularly silent, and when he spoke to either Madelaine or Louise, it was in a softened voice.

Van Heldre looked at his daughter.

Madelaine looked at her father, and they thoroughly read each other's thoughts, the girl's bright gray eyes saying to him as plainly as could be—

"You are quite right."

"Well," said Van Heldre to himself, as he placed a spoonful of black currant jam on his plate, and then over that two piled-up table-spoonfuls of clotted cream—"she's as nice and true-hearted a girl as ever stepped, and Leslie's a man, every inch of him. I'd have said *yes* in a moment if he had wanted my girl. I'm glad of it; but, poor fellow, what he'll have to suffer from that terrible old woman!"

He had just thought this, and was busy composing a *nocturne* or a *diurne*—probably the latter from its tints of red and yellow—upon his plate, which flowed with jam and cream, when Aunt Marguerite, who had eaten all she wished, began to stir her tea with courtly grace, and raised her voice in continuation of something she had been saying, but it was twenty-four hours before.

"Yes, Mr. Pradelle," she said, so that every one should hear; "my memories of the past are painful, and yet a delight. We old Huguenots are proud of our past."

"You must be, madam."

"And you too," said the lady. "I feel sure that if you will take the trouble you will find that I am right. The Pradelles must have been of our people."

"I'll look into it as soon as I get back to town," said the young man.

Harry gave him a very vulgar wink.

"Do," said Aunt Marguerite. "By the way, I don't think I told you that though my brother persists in calling himself Vine, our name is Des Vignes, and we belong to one of the oldest families in Auvergne."

"Yes, that's right, Mr. Pradelle," said the host, nodding pleasantly; "but when a cruel persecution drove us over here, and old England held out her arms to us, and we found a kindly welcome——"

"My dear George!" interposed Aunt Marguerite.

"Let me finish, my dear," said Mr. Vine, good-temperedly. "It's Mr. Pradelle's last evening here."

"For the present, George, for the present."

"Ah, yes, of course, for the present, and I should like him to hear my version too."

Aunt Marguerite tapped the back of her left hand with her fan impatiently.

"We found here a hearty welcome and a home," continued Mr. Vine, "and we said we can never—we will never—return to the land of fire and the sword; and then we, some of us poor, some of us well-to-do, settled down among our English brothers, and thanked God that in this new Land of Canaan we had found rest."

"And my dear Mr. Pradelle," began Aunt Marguerite, hastily; but Mr. Vine was started, and he talked on.

"In time we determined to be, in spite of our French descent, English of the English, for our children's sake, and we worked with them, and traded with them; and, to show our faith in them, and to avoid all further connection and military service in the country we had left, we even anglicized our names. My people became Vines; the D'Aubigneys, Daubney or Dobbs; the Boileaus, Drinkwater;

F 2

the Guipets, Guppy. Vulgarizing our names, some people say; but never mind, we found rest, prosperity, and peace."

"Quite right, Mr. Pradelle," said Van Heldre, "and in spite of my name and my Huguenot descent, I say, thank Heaven I am now an Englishman.'

"No, no, no, no, Mr. Van Heldre," said Aunt Marguerite, throwing herself back, and looking at him with a pitying smile. "You cannot prove your Huguenot descent."

"Won't contradict you, ma'am," said Van Heldre. "Capital jam this, Louise."

"You must be of Dutch descent," said Aunt Marguerite.

"I went carefully over my father's pedigree, Miss Marguerite," said Madelaine quietly.

"Indeed, my child?" said the lady, raising her brows.

"And I found without doubt that the Venelttes fled during the persecutions to Holland, where they stayed for half a century, and changed their names to Van Heldre before coming to England."

"Quite right," said Van Heldre in a low voice. "Capital cream."

"Ah, yes," said Aunt Margaret; "but, my dear child, such papers are often deceptive."

"Yes," said Van Heldre, smiling, "often enough; so are traditions and many of our beliefs about ancestry; but I hope I have enough of what you call the *haute noblesse* in me to give way, and not attempt to argue the point."

"No, Mr. Van Heldre," said Aunt Margaret, with a smile of pity and good-humoured contempt; "we have often argued together upon this question, but I cannot sit in silence and hear you persist in that which is not true. No; you have not any Huguenot blood in your veins."

"My dear madam, I feel at times plethoric enough to wish that the old-fashioned idea of being blooded in the spring were still in vogue. I have so much Huguenot blood in my veins, that I should be glad to have less."

Aunt Margaret shook her head, and tightened her lips.

"Low Dutch," she said to herself, "Low Dutch."

Van Heldre read her thoughts in the movement of her lips.

"Don't much matter," he said. "Vine, old fellow, think I shall turn over a new leaf."

"Eh? New leaf?"

"Yes; get a good piece of marsh, make a

dam to keep out the sea, and take to keeping cows.    What capital cream!"

"Yes, Mr. Pradelle," continued Aunt Margaret; "we are Huguenots of the Huguenots, and it is the dream of my life that Henri should assert his right to the title his father repudiates, and become Comte des Vignes."

"Ah!" said Pradelle.

"Vigorous steps have only to be taken to wrest the family estates in Auvergne from the usurpers who hold them.    I have long fought for this, but so far, I grieve to say, vainly. My brother here has mistaken notions about the respectability of trade, and is content to vegetate."

"Oh, you miserable old vegetable!" said Van Heldre to himself, as he gave his friend a droll look, and shook his head.

"To vegetate in this out-of-the-way place when he should be watching over the welfare of his country, and as a nobleman of that land, striving to stem the tide of democracy. He will not do it; but if I live my nephew Henri shall, as soon as he can be rescued from the degrading influence of trade, and the clerk's stool in an office.    Ah, my poor boy, I pity you, and I say out boldly that I am not surprised that you should have thrown up post after post in disgust, and refused to settle down to such sordid wretchedness."

"My dear Marguerite! our visitors."

"I must speak, George. Mr. Van Heldre loves trade."

"I do, ma'am."

"Therefore he cannot feel with me."

"Well, never mind, my dear. Let some one else be Count des Vignes, only let me be in peace, and don't fill poor Harry's head with that stuff just before he's leaving home to go up to the great city, where he will, I am sure, redeem the follies of the past, and prove himself a true man. Harry, my dear boy, we'll respect Aunt Margaret's opinions; but we will not follow them out. Van, old fellow, Leslie, Mr. Pradelle, a glass of wine. We'll drink Harry's health. All filled? That's right. Harry, my boy, a true honest man is nature's nobleman. God speed you, my boy; and His blessing be upon all your works. Health and happiness to you, my son!"

"Amen," said Van Heldre; and the simple old-fashioned health was drunk.

"Eh, what's that—letters?" said Vine, as a servant entered the room and handed her master three.

"For you, Mr. Pradelle; for you, Harry,

and for me.  May we open them, Mrs. Van
Heldre?  They may be important."

"Of course, Mr. Vine, of course."

Pradelle opened his, glanced at it, and
thrust it into his pocket.

Harry did likewise.

Mr. Vine read his twice, then dropped it
upon the table.

"Papa!—father!" cried Louise, starting
from her place, and running round to him as
he stood up with a fierce angry light in his
eyes, and the table was in confusion.

"Tidings at last of the French estates, Mr.
Pradelle," whispered Aunt Margaret.

"Papa, is anything wrong?  Is it bad
news?" cried Louise.

"Wrong!  Bad news!" he cried, flashing
up from the quiet student to the stern man,
stung to the quick by the announcement he
had just received.  "Van Heldre, old friend,
you know how I strove among our connections
and friends to place him where he might work
and rise and prove himself my son."

"Yes, yes, old fellow, but be calm."

"Father, hush!" whispered Louise, as she
glanced at Leslie's sympathetic countenance.
"Hush!  Be calm!"

"How can I be calm?" cried the old man

fiercely. "The Des Vignes! The family estates! The title! You hear this, Margaret. Here is a fine opportunity for the search to be made—the old castle and the vineyards to be rescued from the occupiers."

"George—brother, what do you mean?" cried the old lady indignantly, and she laid her hand upon her nephew's shoulder, as he sat gazing straight down before him at his plate.

"What do I mean?" cried the indignant father, tossing the letter towards her. "I mean that my son is once more dismissed from his situation in disgrace."

# CHAPTER V.

"Now, sir, have the goodness to tell me what you mean to do."

Harry Vine looked at his father, thrust his hands low down into his pockets, leaned back against the mantelpiece, and was silent.

Vine senior leaned over a shallow glass jar, with a thin splinter of wood in his hand, upon which he had just impaled a small fragment of raw, minced periwinkle, and this he thrust down to where a gorgeous sea-anemone sat spread open upon a piece of rock—chipped from out of one of the caverns on the coast.

The anemone's tentacles bristled all around, giving the creature the aspect of a great flower; and down among these the scrap of food was thrust till it touched them, when the tentacles began to curve over, and draw the scrap of shell-fish down toward the large central mouth, in which it soon began to disappear.

Vine senior looked up.

"I have done everything I could for you in the way of education. I have, I am sure, been a most kind and indulgent father. You have had a liberal supply of money, and by the exercise of my own and the personal interest of friends, I have obtained for you posts among our people, any one of which was the beginning of prosperity and position, such as a youth should have been proud to win."

"But they were so unsuitable, father. All connected with trade."

"Shame, Harry! As if there was anything undignified in trade. No matter whether it be trade or profession by which a man honestly earns his subsistence, it is an honourable career. And yet five times over you have been thrown back on my hands in disgrace."

"Well, I can't help it, father; I've done my best."

"Your best!" cried Vine senior, taking up a glass rod, and stirring the water in another glass jar. "It is not true."

"But it's so absurd. You're a rich man."

"If I were ten times as well off, I would not have you waste your life in idleness. You are not twenty-four, and I am determined that you shall take some post. I have seen too much of what follows when a restless, idle young man sits down to wait for his father's money. There, I am busy now. Go and think over what I have said. You must and shall do something. It is now a month since I received that letter. What is Mr. Pradelle doing down here again?"

"Come for a change, as any other gentleman would."

"Gentleman?"

"Well, he has a little income of his own, I suppose. If I've been unlucky that's no reason why I should throw over my friends."

The father looked at the son in a perplexed way, and then fed another sea-anemone, Harry looking on contemptuously.

"Well, sir, you have heard what I said. Go and think it over."

"Yes, father."

The young man left the business-like study, and encountered his sister in the hall.

"Well, Harry?"

"Well, Lou."

"What does papa say?"

"The old story. I'm to go back to drudgery. I think I shall enlist."

"For shame! and you professing to care as you do for Madelaine."

"So I do. I worship her."

"Then prove it by exerting yourself in the way papa wishes. I wonder you have not more spirit."

"And I wonder you have not more decency towards my friends."

Louise coloured slightly.

"Here you profess to believe in my going into trade and drudging behind a counter."

"I did not know that a counter had ever been in question, Harry," said his sister sarcastically.

"Well, a clerk's desk; it's all the same. I believe you would like to see me selling tea and sugar."

"I don't think I should mind."

"No; that's it. I'm to be disgraced while you are so much of the fine lady that you look down on, and quite insult, my friend Pradelle."

"Aunt Margaret wishes to speak to you, dear," said Louise gravely. "I promised to tell you as soon as you left the study."

"Then hang it all! why didn't you tell me? Couldn't resist a chance for a lecture. There's only one body here who understands me, and that's aunt. Why even Madelaine's turning against me now, and I believe it is all your doing."

"I have done nothing but what is for your good, Harry."

"Then you own to it? You have been talking to Maddy?"

"She came and confided in me, and I believe I spoke the truth."

"Yes, I knew it!" cried Harry warmly. "Then look here, my lady, I'm not blind. I've petted you and been the best of brothers, but if you turn against me I shall turn against you."

"Harry dear!"

"Ah, that startles you, does it? Then I shall tell the truth, and I'll back up Aunt Margaret through thick and thin."

"What do you mean?"

"What Aunt Margaret says. That long Scotch copper-miner is no match for you."

"Harry!"

"And I shall tell him this, if he comes hanging about here where he sees he is not wanted, and stands in the way of a gentleman of good French Huguenot descent, I'll horsewhip him. There!"

He turned on his heel, and bounded up the old staircase three steps at a time.

"Oh!" ejaculated Louise, as she stood till she heard a sharp tap at her aunt's door and her brother enter, and close it after him. "Mr. Pradelle, too, of all people in the world!"

"Ah, my darling," cried Aunt Margaret, looking up from the tambour-frame and smoothing out the folds of her antique flowered peignoir. "Bring that stool, and come and sit down."

Harry bent down and kissed her rather sulkily. Then in a half-contemptuous way he fetched the said stool, embroidered by the lady herself, and placed it at her feet.

"Sit down, my dear."

Harry lowered himself into a very uncomfortable position, while Aunt Margaret placed one arm about his neck, struck a graceful pose, and began to smooth over the young man's already too smooth hair.

"I want to have another very serious talk with you, my boy," she said. "Ah, yes," she continued, raising his chin and looking down in his disgusted face: "how every lineament shows your descent!"

"I say, aunt, I've just brushed my hair."

"Yes, dear, but you should not hide your forehead. It is the brow of the Des Vignes."

"Oh, all right, auntie, have it your own way. But, I say, have you got any money?

" Alas ! no, my boy."

"I don't mean now. I mean haven't you really got any to leave me in your will ? "

There was a far-off look in Aunt Margaret's eyes as she slowly shook her head.

" You will leave me what you have, aunt ? "

" If I had hundreds of thousands, you should have all, Henri ; but, alas, I have none. I had property once."

" What became of it ? "

" Well, my dear, it is a long story and a sad one. I could not tell it to you even in brief, but you are a man now, and must know the meaning of the word love."

" Oh, yes, I know what that means ; but I say, don't fidget my hair about so."

" I could not tell you all, Henri. It was thirty years ago. He was a French gentleman of noble descent. His estates had been confiscated, and I was only too glad to place my little fortune at his disposal to recover them."

" And did he ? "

" No, my dear. Those were terrible times. He lost all ; and with true nobility, he wrote to me that he loved me too well to drag me down to poverty—to share his lot as an exile.

I have never seen him since. But I would have shared his lot."

"Humph! Lost it? Then if I had money and tried for our family estates, I might lose it too."

"No, no, my boy; you would be certain to win. Did you do what I told you?"

"Yes, aunt; but I can't use them down here."

"Let me look, my dear; and I do not see why not. You must be bold; and proud of your descent."

"But they'd laugh."

"Let them," said Aunt Margaret grandly. "By and by they will bow down. Let me see."

The young man took a card-case from his pocket, on which was stamped in gold a French count's coronet.

"Ah! yes; that is right," said the old lady, snatching the case with trembling fingers, opening it, and taking out a card on which was also printed a coronet. "*Comte Henri des Vignes,*" she read, in an excited manner, and with tears in her eyes. "My darling boy!"

"Cost a precious lot, aunt; made a regular hole in your diamond ring."

"Did you sell it?"

" No ; Vic Pradelle pawned it for me."

"Ah! he is a friend of whom you may be proud, Henri."

"Not a bad sort of fellow, aunt. He got precious little on the ring, though, and I spent it nearly all."

"Never mind the ring, my boy, and I'm very glad you have the cards. Now for a little serious talk about the future."

" Wish to goodness there was no future," said Harry glumly.

" Would you like to talk about the past, then ?" said the old lady playfully.

" Wish there was no past neither," grumbled Harry.

" Then we will talk about the present, my dear, and about—let me whisper to you—love ! "

She placed her thin lips close to her nephew's ear, and then held him at arm's length and smiled upon him proudly.

"Love! Too expensive a luxury for me, auntie. I say, you are ruffling my hair so."

" Too expensive, Henri ? No, my darling boy ; follow my advice, and the richest and fairest of the daughters of France shall sue for your hand."

"I say, auntie," he said laughingly, "aren't you laying on the colour rather thick?"

"Not a bit, my darling; and that's why I want to talk to you about your sister's friend."

"What, Maddy?" he said eagerly; "then you approve of it."

"Approve! Pah! you are jesting, my dear. I approve of your making an alliance with a fat Dutch fraulein!"

"Oh, come, aunt!" said Harry, looking nettled; "Madelaine is not Dutch, nor yet fat."

"I know better, my boy. Dutch! Dutch! Dutch! Look at her father and her mother! No, my boy, you could not make an alliance with a girl like that. She might do for a kitchen-maid."

"Auntie!"

"Silly boy!"

"And she'll be rich some day."

"If she were heiress to millions she could not marry you. As some writer says, eagles do not mate with plump Dutch ducklings. No, Henri, my boy, you must wait."

Harry frowned.

"That is a boyish piece of nonsense, un-worthy the Comte dés Vignes, my dear boy.

But tell me—you have been with your father
—what does he say now ? ”

“ The old story.   I must go to work.”

“ Poor George !” sighed Aunt Margaret ;
“ always so sordid in his ideas in early life :
now that he is wealthy so utterly wanting
in aspirations !   Always dallying over some
miserable shrimp.   He has no more ambition
than one of those silly fish over which he
sits and dreams.   Oh, Henri, my boy, when
I look back at what our family has been—
right back into the distant ages of French
history—valorous knights and noble ladies ;
and later on, how they graced the court
at banquet and at ball, I weep the salt
tears of misery to see my brother sink so
low.”

“ Ah ! well, it’s of no use, aunt.   I must
go and turn somebody’s grindstone again.”

“ No, Henri, it shall not be,” cried the old
lady, with flashing eyes.   “ We must think ;
we must plot and plan.”

“ If you please, ma’am, I’ve brought your
lunch,” said a voice ; and Liza, the maid, who
bore a strong resemblance to the fish-woman
who had accosted Uncle Luke at the mouth
of the harbour, set down a delicately-cooked
cutlet and bit of fish, all spread on a snowy

napkin, with the accompaniments of plate, glass, and a decanter of sherry.

"Ah! yes, my lunch," said Aunt Margaret, with a sigh. "Go, and think over what I have said, my dear, and we will talk again another time."

"All right, auntie," said the young man, rising slowly; "but it seems to me as if the best thing I could do would be to jump into the sea."

"No, no, Henri," said Aunt Margaret, taking up a silver spoon and shaking it slowly at her nephew, "a Des Vignes was ready with his sword in defence of his honour, and to advance his master's cause; but he never dreamed of taking his own life. That, my dear, would be the act of one of the low-born *canaille*. Remember who you are, and wait. I am working for you, and you shall triumph yet. Consult your friend."

"Sometimes I think it's all gammon," said Harry, as he went slowly down-stairs, and out into the garden, "and sometimes it seems as if it would be very jolly. I dare say the old woman is right, and——"

"What are you talking about—muttering aside like the wicked man on the stage?"

"Hullo, Vic! You there?"

"Yes, dear boy. I'm here for want of somewhere better."

"Consult your friend!" Aunt Margaret's last words.

"Been having a cigar?"

"I've been hanging about here this last hour. How is it she hasn't been for a walk?"

"Louie? Don't know. Here, let's go down under the cliff, and have a talk over a pipe."

"The latter, if you like; never mind the former. Yes, I will; for I want a few words of a sort."

"What about?" said Harry, as they strolled away.

"Everything. Look here, old fellow; we've been the best of chums ever since you shared my desk."

"Yes, and you shared my allowance."

"Well chums always do. Then I came down with you, and it was all as jolly as could be, and I was making way fast, in spite of that confounded red-headed porridge-eating fellow. Then came that upset, and I went away. Then you wrote to me in answer to my letter about having a good thing on, and said 'Come down.'"

"And you came," said Harry thoughtfully, "and the good thing turned out a bad thing, as every one does that I join in."

"Well, that was an accident; speculators must have some crust as well as crumb."

"But I get all crust."

"No, I seem to be getting all crust now from your people. Your aunt's right enough, but your father casts his cold shoulder and stale bread at me whenever we meet; and as for a certain lady, she regularly cut me yesterday."

"Well, I can't help that, Vic. You know what I said when you told me you were on that. I said that I couldn't do anything, and that I wouldn't do anything if I could; but that I wouldn't stand in your way if you liked to try."

"Yes, I know what you said," grumbled Pradelle, as they strolled down to the shore, went round the rocks, and then strolled on over and amongst the shingle and sand, till— a suitable spot presenting itself, about half a mile from the town—they sat down on the soft sand, tilted their hats over their eyes, leaned their backs against a huge stone, and then lit up and began to smoke.

"You see it's like this," said Pradelle;

" I know I'm not much of a catch, but I like her, and that ought to make up for a great deal."

" Yes."

"She don't know her own mind, that's about it," continued Pradelle; "and a word from you might do a deal."

" Got any money, Vic?"

" Now there's a mean sort of a question to ask a friend! Have I got any money? As if a man must be made of money before he may look at his old chum's sister."

" I wasn't thinking about her, but of something else," said Harry hastily.

"Ah, well, I wasn't; but look there!"

"What at?" said Harry, whose eyes were shut, and his thoughts far away.

"Them. They're going for a walk. Why, Hal, old chap, they saw us come down here."

Harry started into wakefulness, and realized the fact that his sister and Madelaine Van Heldre were passing before them, but down by the water's edge.

"Let's follow them," said Pradelle eagerly.

" Wait a moment."

Harry waited to think, and scraps of his aunt's remarks floated through his brain respecting the fair daughters of France, who would fall at the feet of the young count.

Harry cogitated. The daughters of France were no doubt very lovely, but they were imaginative; and though Madelaine Van Heldre might, as his aunt said, not be of the pure Huguenot blood, still that fact did not seem to matter to him. For that was not imagination before him, but the bright, natural, clever girl whom he had known from childhood, his old playfellow, who had always seemed to supply a something wanting in his mental organization, the girl who had led him and influenced his career.

"Bother Aunt Marguerite!" he said to himself, and then aloud, " Come along!"

# CHAPTER VI.

HARRY VINE SPEAKS PLAINLY; SO DOES HIS
FRIEND.

LOUISE and Madelaine went on down by
the water's edge, in profound ignorance of the
fact that they were followed at a distance of
about a couple of hundred yards.

The two friends female were then in profound ignorance of the fact that they were
watched, so were the two friends male.

For some time past the owner of the mine
high up on the cliff had been a thoroughly
energetic man of business, but after the first
introduction to the Vine family his business
energy seemed to receive an impetus. He
was working for her, everything might be for
her.

Then came Pradelle upon the scene, and
the young Scot was not long in seeing that
the brother's London friend was also impressed,
and that his advances found favour with

Harry.   Whether they did with the sister he could not tell.

The consequence was that there was a good deal of indecision on Duncan Leslie's part, some neglect of his busy mine, and a good deal of use of a double glass, which was supposed to be kept in a room, half office, half study and laboratory, for the purpose of scanning the shipping coming into port.

On the day in question the glass was being applied to a purpose rather reprehensible, perhaps, but with some excuse of helping Duncan Leslie's affair of the heart.   From his window he could see the old granite-built house, and with interruptions, due to rocks and doublings and jutting pieces of cliff, a great deal of the winding and zigzag path, half steps, which led down to the shore.

As, then, was frequently the case, the glass was directed toward the residence of the Vines, and Duncan Leslie saw Louise and Madelaine go down to the sea, stand watching the receding tide, and then go off west.

After gazing through the glass for a time he laid it down, with his heart beating faster than usual, as he debated within himself whether he should go down to the shore and follow them.

It was a hard fight, and inclination was rapidly mastering etiquette, when two figures, hitherto concealed, came into view from beneath the cliff and began to follow the ladies.

Duncan Leslie's eyes flashed as he caught up the glass again, and after looking through it for a few minutes he closed it and threw it down.

"I'm making a fool of myself," he said bitterly. "Better attend to my business and think about it no more."

The desire was upon him to focus the glass again and watch what took place, but he turned away with an angry ejaculation and put the glass in its case.

"I might have known better," he said, "and it would be like playing the spy."

He strode out and went to his engine-house, forcing himself to take an interest in what was going on, and wishing the while that he had not used that glass in so reprehensible a way.

Oddly enough, just at that moment Uncle Luke was seated outside the door of his little cottage in its niche of the cliff below the mine, and wishing for this very glass.

His was a cottage of the roughest construc-

tion, which he had bought some years before
of an old fisherman; and his seat—he could
not afford chairs, he said—was a rough block
of granite, upon which he was very fond of
sunning himself when the weather was fine.

"I've a good mind to go and ask Leslie to
lend me his glass," muttered the old man.
"No. He'd only begin asking favours of me.
But all that ought to be stopped. Wonder
whether George knows. What's Van Heldre
about? As for those two girls, I'll give them
such a talking to—the gipsies! Bah! it's
no business of mine! I'm not going to
marry."

"Yes, let's sit down," said Madelaine, turning round. "Oh!"

"What is it? sprained your ankle?"

"No. Mr. Pradelle and Harry are close by."

"Let's walk on quickly then, and go round
back by the fields."

"But it will be six miles."

"Never mind if it's sixteen," said Louise,
increasing her pace.

"Hallo, girls," cried Harry, and they were
obliged to face round.

There was no warm look of welcome from
either, but Pradelle was too much of the
London man of the world to be taken aback,

and he stepped forward to Louise's side, smiling.

"You have chosen a delightful morning for your walk, Miss Vine."

"Yes, but we were just going back."

"No; don't go back yet," said Harry quickly, for he had strung himself up. "Vic, old fellow, walk on with my sister. I want to have a chat with Miss Van Heldre."

The girls exchanged glances, each seeming to ask the other for counsel.

Then, in a quiet, decisive way, Madelaine spoke.

"Yes, do, Louie dear; I wanted to speak to your brother, too."

There was another quick look passing between the friends, and then Louise bowed and walked on, Pradelle giving Harry a short nod which meant, according to his judgment, "It's all right."

Louise was for keeping close to her companion, but her brother evidently intended her to have a *tête-à-tête* encounter with his friend, and she realized directly that Madelaine did not second her efforts. In fact the latter yielded at once to Harry's manœuvres, and hung back with him, while Pradelle pressed forward, so that before many minutes had elapsed, the couples, as they walked west, were separated by a space of quite a couple of hundred yards.

"Now I do call that good of you, Maddy," said Harry eagerly. "You are, and you always were, a dear good little thing."

"Do you think so?" she said directly, and her pleasant bright face was now very grave.

"Do I think so! You know I do. There, I want a good talk with you, dear. It's time I spoke plainly, and that we fully understood one another."

"I thought we did, Harry."

"Well, yes, of course, but I want to be more plain. We're no boy and girl now."

"No, Harry, we have grown up to be man and woman."

"Yes, and ever since we were boy and girl, Maddy, I've loved you very dearly."

Madelaine turned her clear searching eyes upon him in the most calm and untroubled way.

"Yes, Harry, you have always seemed to."

"And you have always cared for me very much?"

"Yes, Harry. Always."

"Well, don't say it in such a cold, serious way, dear."

" But it is a matter upon which one is bound to be cool and very serious."

" Well, yes, of course. I don't know that people are any the better for showing a lot of gush."

" No, Harry, it is not so deep as the liking which is calm and cool and enduring."

" I s'pose not," said the young man very disconcertedly. " But don't be quite so cool. I know you too well to think you would play with me."

" I hope I shall always be very sincere, Harry."

" Of course you will. I know you will. We began by being playmates—almost like brother and sister."

" Yes, Harry."

" But I always felt as I grew older that I should some day ask you to be my darling little wife; and, come now, you always thought so too ? "

" Yes, Harry, I always thought so too."

" Ah, that's right, dear," said the young man, flushing. " You always were the dearest and most honest and plain-spoken girl I ever met."

" I try to be."

" Of course ; and look yonder, there's old

Pradelle, the dearest and best friend a fellow
ever had, talking to Louie as I'm talking to
you."

"Yes, I'm afraid he is."

"Afraid? Oh, come now, don't be prejudiced. I want you to like Victor."

"That would be impossible."

"Impossible! What, the man who will
most likely be Louie's husband?"

"Mr. Pradelle will never be Louie's husband."

"What! Why, how do you know?"

"Because I know your sister's heart too
well."

"And you don't like Pradelle?"

"No, Harry; and I'm sorry you ever chose
him for a companion."

"Oh, come, dear, that's prejudice and a bit
of jealousy. Well, never mind about that
now. I want to talk about ourselves."

"Yes, Harry."

"I want you to promise to be my little
wife. I'm four-and-twenty, and you are
nearly twenty, so it's quite time to talk
about it."

Madelaine shook her head.

"Oh, come!" he said merrily, "no girl's
coyness: we are too old friends for that, and

understand one another too well. Come, dear,
when is it to be ?"

She turned and looked in the handsome
flushed face beside her, and then said in the
most cool and matter-of-fact way :

"It is too soon to talk like that, Harry."

"Too soon ?  Not a bit of it.  You have
told me that you will be my wife."

"Some day, perhaps."

"Oh, nonsense, dear !  I've been thinking
this all over well.  You see, Maddy, you've
let my not sticking to business 'trouble
you."

"Yes, Harry, very much."

"Well, I'm very sorry, dear ; and I suppose
I have been a bit to blame, but I've been
doing distasteful work, and I've been like a
boat swinging about without an anchor.  I
want you to be my anchor to hold me fast.
I've wanted something to steady me—something to work for ; and if I've got you for a
wife I shall be a different man directly."

Madelaine sighed.

"Aunt Marguerite won't like it, because she
is not very fond of you."

"No," said Madelaine, "she does not like
fat Dutch frauleins—Dutch dolls."

"Get out !  What stuff !  She's a prejudiced

old woman full of fads.  She never did like you."

" Never, Harry."

" Well, that doesn't matter a bit."

" No.   That does not matter a bit."

" You see I've had no end of thinks about all this, and it seems to me that if we're married at once, it will settle all the worries and bothers I've had lately.  The governor wants me to go to business again ; but what's the use of that ?  He's rich, and so is your father, and they can easily supply us with all that we should want, and then we shall be as happy as can be.  Of course I shall work at something.  I don't believe in a fellow with nothing to do.  You don't either ? "

" No, Harry."

" Of course not, but all that toiling and moiling for the sake of money is a mistake. Never mind what Aunt Marguerite says.  I'll soon work her round, and of course I can do what I like with the governor.  He's so fond of you that he'll be delighted, and he knows it will do me good.  So now there's nothing to do but for me to go and see your father and ask his consent.  I did think of letting you coax him round : but that would be cowardly, wouldn't it ? "

H 2

"Yes, Harry, very cowardly, and lower you very much in my eyes."

"Of course : but, I say, don't be so serious. Well, it's a bitter pill to swallow, for your governor will be down on me tremendously. I'll face him, though. I'll talk about our love and all that sort of thing, and it will be all right. I'll go to him to-day."

"No, Harry," said Madelaine, looking him full in the face, "don't do that."

"Why ? "

"Because it would expose you to a very severe rebuff."

"Will you speak to him then ? No : I'll do it."

"No. If you did my father would immediately speak to me, and I should have to tell him what I am going to tell you."

"Well ? Out with it."

"Do you suppose," said Madelaine, once more turning her clear frank eyes upon the young man, and speaking with a quiet decision that startled him ; "do you suppose I could be so wanting in duty to those at home, so wanting in love to you, Harry, that I could consent to a marriage which would only mean fixing you permanently in your present thoughtless ways ?"

" Madelaine ! "

" Let me finish, Harry, and tell you what has been on my lips for months past.  I am younger by several years than you, but do you think I am so wanting in worldly experience that I am blind to your reckless folly, or the pain you are giving father and sister by your acts ? "

" Why, Maddy," he cried, in a voice full of vexation, which belied the mocking laugh upon his lips, " I didn't think you could preach like that."

" It is time to preach, Harry, when I see you so lost to self-respect, and find that you are ready to place yourself and the girl you wish to call wife, in a dependent position, instead of proudly and manfully making yourself your own master."

" Well, this is pleasant !  Am I to understand that you throw me over ? "

" No, Harry," said Madelaine sadly, " you are to understand that I care for you too much to encourage you in a weak folly."

" A weak folly—to ask you what you have always expected I should ask ! "

" Yes, to ask it at such a time when, after being placed in post after post by my father's help, and losing them one by one by your folly, you——"

"Oh, come, that will do," cried the young man angrily; "if it's to be like this it's a good job that we came to an explanation at once. So this is gentle, amiable, sweet-tempered Madelaine, eh! Hallo! You!"

He turned sharply. Louise and Pradelle had come over a stretch of sand with their footsteps inaudible.

"It is quite time we returned, Madelaine," said Louise gravely; and without another word the two girls walked away.

"'Pon my word," cried Harry with a laugh, "things are improving. Well, Vic, how did you get on?"

"How did I get on indeed!" cried Pradelle angrily. "Look here, Harry ₁Vine, are you playing square with me?"

"What do you mean?"

"What I say: are you honest, or have you been setting her against me?"

"Why you——no, I won't quarrel," cried Harry. "What did she say to you?"

"Say to me? I was never so snubbed in my life. Her ladyship doesn't know me if she thinks I'm going to give up like that."

"There, that'll do, Vic. No threats, please."

"Oh, no; I'm not going to threaten. I can wait."

"Yes," said Harry, thoughtfully; "we chose the wrong time. We mustn't give up, Vic; we shall have to wait."

And they went back to their old nook beneath the cliff to smoke their pipes, while as the thin blue vapour arose Harry's hot anger grew cool, and he began to think of his aunt's words, of Comte Henri des Vignes, and of the fair daughters of France—a reverie from which he was aroused by his companion, as he said suddenly—

"I say, Harry, lad, I want you to lend me a little coin."

# CHAPTER VII.

## CHEZ VAN HELDRE.

THE two friends parted at the gate, Madelaine refusing to go in.

"No," she said; "they will be expecting me at home."

"Maddy dear, ought we not to confide in each other?"

"Ah!" exclaimed Madelaine, with a sigh of relief that the constraint was over. "Yes, dear. Did Mr. Pradelle propose to you?"

"Yes."

"And you told him it was impossible?"

"Yes. What did my brother want to say?"

"That we ought to be married now, and it would make him a better man."

"And you told him it was impossible?"

"Yes."

There was another sigh as if of relief on both sides, and the two girls kissed again and parted.

It was a brisk quarter of an hour's walk to the Van Heldres', which lay at the end of the main street up the valley down which the little river ran; and on entering the door, with a longing upon her to go at once to her room and sit down and cry, Madelaine uttered a sigh full of misery, for she saw that it was impossible.

As she approached the great stone porch leading into the broad hall, which was one of the most attractive-looking places in the house, filled as it was with curiosities and other objects brought by the various captains from the Mediterranean, and embracing cabinets from Constantinople with rugs and pipes, little terra-cotta figures from Sardinia, and pictures and pieces of statuary from Rome, Naples, and Trieste, she was saluted with—

"Ah, my dear, I'm so glad you've come back. Where's papa?"

"I have not seen him, mamma."

"Busy, I suppose. How he does work!" Then suddenly, "By the way, that Mr. Pradelle. I don't like him, my dear."

"Neither do I, mamma."

"That's right, my dear; I'm very glad to hear you say so; but surely Louie Vine is not going to be beguiled by him?"

"Oh no."

"Ah, that's all very well; but Luke Vine came in as he went by, to say in his sneering fashion that Louie and Mr. Pradelle were down on the shore, and that you were walking some distance behind with Harry."

"Mr. Luke Vine seems to have plenty of time for watching his neighbours," said Madelaine contemptuously.

"Yes; he is always noticing things; but don't blame him, dear. I'm sure he means well, and I can forgive him anything for that. Here's your father."

"Ah! my dears," said Van Heldre cheerily. "Tired out."

"You must be," said Mrs. Van Heldre, bustling about him to take his hat and gloves. "Here, do come and sit down."

The merchant went into the drawing-room very readily, and submitted to several little pleasant attentions from wife and daughter.

Evening came on with Van Heldre seated in his easy-chair, thoughtfully watching wife and daughter; both of whom had work in their laps; but Mrs. Van Heldre's was all a pretence, for, after a few stitches, her head began to nod forward, then back against the cushion, and then, as if by magic, she was fast asleep.

Madelaine's needle, however, flew fast, and she went on working, with her father watching her attentively, till she raised her eyes.

" You want to say something to me, Maddy," he said in a low voice.

" Yes, papa."

" About your walk down on the beach ? "

Madelaine nodded.

" You know I went."

" Yes ; I saw you, and Luke Vine came and told me as well."

" It was very kind of him," said Madelaine, with a touch of sarcasm in her voice.

" Kind and unkind, my dear. You see he has no business—nothing to do but to think of other people. But he means well, my dear, and he likes you."

" I have often thought so."

" Yes ; and you were right. He warned me that I was not to let your intimacy grow closer with his nephew."

" Indeed, papa ! "

" Yes, my dear. He said that I was a—— well, I will not tell you what, for not stopping it directly, for that Harry was rapidly drifting into a bad course—that it was a hopeless case."

" That is not the way to redeem him, father."

"No, my dear, it is not. But you were going to say something to me?"

"Yes," said Madelaine, hesitating. Then putting down her work she rose and went to her father's side, knelt down, and resting her arms upon his knees, looked straight up in his face.

"Well, Maddy?"

"I wanted to speak to you about Harry."

There was a slight twitching about the merchant's brows, but his face was calm directly, and he said coolly—

"What about Harry Vine?"

Madelaine hesitated for a few moments, and then spoke out firmly and bravely.

"I have been thinking about his position, father, and of how sad it is for him to be wasting his days as he is down here."

"Very sad, Maddy. He is, as Luke Vine says, going wrong. Well?"

"I have been thinking, papa, that you might take him into your office and give him a chance of redeeming the past."

"Nice suggestion, my dear. What would old Crampton say?"

"Mr. Crampton could only say that you had done a very kind act for the son of your old friend."

"Humph! Well?"

" You could easily arrange to take him, papa, and with your firm hand over him it would do an immense deal of good."

" Not to me."

There was a pause, and Van Heldre gazed into his child's unblenching eyes.

" So we are coming at facts," he said at last. " Harry asked you to interfere on his behalf?"

Madelaine shook her head and smiled.

" Is this your own idea?"

" Entirely."

" Then what was the meaning of the walk on the beach to-day?"

" Harry sought for it, and said that we had been playfellows from children, that he loved me very dearly, and he asked me to be his wife."

" The——"

Van Heldre checked himself.

" And what did you say?"

" That it was impossible."

" Then you do not care for him?"

Madelaine was silent.

" Then you do not care for him?"

" I'm afraid I care for him very much indeed," said Madelaine firmly.

" Let me thoroughly understand you, my darling. You love George Vine's son—your old friend's brother ? "

" Yes, father," said Madelaine, in a voice little above a whisper.

" And he has asked you to be his wife ? "

" Yes."

" Tell me what answer you gave him."

" That I would never marry a man so wanting in self-respect."

" Hah ! "

" He said that our parents were rich, that there was no need for him to toil as he had done, but that if I consented it would give him an impetus to work."

" And you declined conditionally ? "

" I declined absolutely, father."

" And yet you love him ? "

" I'm afraid I love him very dearly."

" You are a strange girl, Madelaine."

" Yes, father."

" Do you know what it means for me to take this fellow into my office ? "

" Much trouble and care."

" Yes. Then why should I ? "

" Because, as you have so often taught me, we cannot live for ourselves alone. Because he is the son of your very old friend."

" Yes," said Van Heldre softly.

" Because it might save him from a downward course now that there is, I believe, a crisis in his life."

" And because you love him, Maddy ? "

She answered with a look.

" And if I were so insane, so quixotic, as to do all this, what guarantee have I that he would not gradually lead you to think differently— to consent to be his wife before he had redeemed his character ? "

" The trust you have in me."

" Hah ! " ejaculated Van Heldre again. And there was another long silence.

" I feel that I must plead for him, father. You could influence him so much."

" I'm afraid not, my child. If he has not the manliness to do what is right for your sake, anything I could do or say would not be of much avail."

" You underrate your power, father," said Madelaine, with a look full of pride in him.

" And if I did this I might have absolute confidence that matters should go no farther until he had completely changed ? "

" You know you might."

" Hah ! " sighed Van Heldre.

" You will think this over, father ? "

"There is no need, my dear."

"No need?"

"No, my child. I have for some days past been thinking over this very thing, just in the light in which you placed it."

"You have?"

"Yes, and I had a long talk with George Vine this afternoon respecting his son."

"Oh, father!"

"I told him I could see that the trouble was growing bigger and telling upon him, and proposed that I should take Harry here."

Madelaine had started to her feet.

"Presuming that he does not refuse after his father has made my proposals known, Harry Vine comes here daily to work."

Madelaine's arms were round her father's neck.

"You have made me feel very happy and satisfied, my dear, and may Heaven speed what is going to be a very arduous task."

Just then Mrs. Van Heldre raised her head and looked round.

"Bless my heart!" she exclaimed. "I do believe I have nearly been to sleep."

# CHAPTER VIII.

"HALLO, Scotchman!"

"Hallo, Eng——I mean French—— What am I to call you, Mr. Luke Vine?"

"Englishman, of course."

Uncle Luke was seated, in a very shabby-looking gray tweed Norfolk jacket made long, a garment which suited his tastes, from its being an easy comfortable article of attire. He had on an old Panama hat, a good deal stained, and had a thick stick armed with a strong iron point useful for walking among the rocks, and upon this staff he rested as he sat outside his cottage door watching the sea and pondering as to the probability of a shoal of fish being off the point.

His home with its tiny scrap of rough walled-in garden, which grew nothing but sea holly and tamarisk, was desolate-looking in the extreme, but the view therefrom of the half natural pier sheltering the vessels in the harbour of the twin town was glorious.

He had had his breakfast and taken his seat out in the sunshine, when he became aware of the fact that Duncan Leslie was coming down from the mine buildings above, and he hailed him with a snarl and the above words.

" Glorious morning."

" Humph! Yes, but what's that got to do with you ? "

" Everything. Do you suppose I don't like fine weather ? "

" I thought you didn't care for anything but money grubbing."

" Then you were mistaken, because I do."

" Nonsense! You think of nothing but copper, spoiling the face of nature with the broken rubbish your men dig out of the bowels of the earth, poisoning the air with the fumes of those abominable furnaces. Look at that ! "

The old man raised his stick and made a vicious dig with it in the direction of the mine.

" Look at what ? "

" That shaft. Looks like some huge worm that your men disturbed down below, and sent

it crawling along the hill slope till it could rear
its abominable head in the air and look which
way to go to be at rest."

" It was there when I took the mine, and it
answers its purpose."

" Bah ! What purpose ? To make money ? "

" Yes ; to make money. Very useful thing,
Mr. Luke."

" Rubbish ! You're as bad as Van Heldre
with his ships and his smelting works. Money !
Money ! Money ! Always money, morning,
noon, and night. One constant hunt for the
accursed stuff. Look at me ! "

" I was looking at you, old fellow ; and
studying you."

" Humph ! Waste of time, unless you follow
my example."

" Then it will be waste of time, sir, for I
certainly shall not follow your example."

" Why not, boy ? Look at me. I have no
troubles. I pay no rent. My wants are few.
I am nearly independent of tradespeople and
tax men. I've no slatternly wife to worry
me, no young children to be always tumbling down the rocks or catching the measles.
I'm free of all these troubles, and I'm a happy
man."

" Well, then, your appearance belies you,

sir, for you do not look it," said Leslie laughing.

"Never you mind my appearance," said Uncle Luke sharply. "I am happy; at least, I should be, if you'd do away with that great smoky chimney and stop those rattling stamps."

"Then I'm afraid that I cannot oblige you, neighbour."

"Humph! Neighbour!"

"I fancy that an unbiassed person would blame you and not me."

"Of course he would."

"He'd say if a man chooses to turn himself into a sort of modern Diogenes——"

"Diogenes be hanged, sir! All a myth. I don't believe there ever was such a body. And look here, Leslie, I imitate no man—no myth. I prefer to live this way for my own satisfaction, and I shall."

"And welcome for me, old fellow; only don't scold me for living my way."

"Not going to. Here, stop! I want to talk to you. How's copper?"

"Up a good deal, but you don't want to know."

"Of course I don't. But look here. What do you think of my nephew?"

" Tall, good-looking young fellow."

" Humph ! What's the good of that ?  You know all about him, of course ? "

" I should prefer not to sit in judgment on the gentleman in question."

" So I suppose.   Nice boy, though, isn't he ? "

Leslie was silent.

" I say he's a nice boy, isn't he ? " cried the old man, raising his voice.

" I heard what you said.  He is your nephew."

" Worse luck !  How is he getting on at Van Heldre's ? "

" I have not the least idea, sir."

" More have I.  They won't tell me.  How about that friend of his ?  What do you think of him ? "

" Really, Mr. Vine," said Leslie, laughing, " I do not set up as a judge of young men's character.  It is nothing to me."

" Yes, it is.  Do you suppose I'm blind ? Do you suppose I can't tell which way the wind blows ?  If I were young, do you know what I should do ? "

" Do away with the chimney-shaft and the stamps," said Leslie, laughing.

" No ; I should just get hold of that fellow

some night, and walk him to where the coach starts."

Leslie's face looked warm.

"And then I should say, 'Jump up, and when you get to the station, book for London; and if ever you show your face in Hakemouth again I'll break your neck.'"

"You must excuse me, Mr. Luke; I'm busy this morning," said Leslie, and he began to descend the steep path.

"Touched him on the tender place," said Uncle Luke, with a chuckle. "Humph! wonder whether Louie will come and see me to-day."

Duncan Leslie went on down the zigzag cliff-path leading from the Wheal Germains copper-mine to the town. It was a picturesque way, with a fresh view at every turn west and east; and an advanced member of the town board had proposed and carried the suggestion of placing rough granite seats here and there in the best parts for resting those who climbed, and for giving others attractive places for sunning themselves and looking out to sea.

About half-way down Leslie passed an invalid, who had taken possession of a seat, and was gazing right away south, and dreaming of lands where the sun always shone—wondering whether the bright maiden Health could be found there.

Lower still Leslie was going on thoughtfully, pondering on Uncle Luke's hints, when the blood suddenly flushed into his cheeks, his heart began to beat rapidly, and he increased his pace. For there unmistakably were two ladies going down the zigzag, and there were no two others in Hakemouth could be mistaken for them.

He hurried on to overtake them. Then he checked himself.

"Where had they been?"

His sinking heart suggested that they had been on their way to visit Uncle Luke, but that they had caught sight of him, and in consequence returned.

His brow grew gloomy, and he walked slowly on, when the blood flushed to his cheeks again, as if he had been surprised in some guilty act, for a sharp voice said—

"No, Mr. Leslie; you would not be able to overtake them now."

He stopped short, and turned to the warm sheltered nook among the rocks where Aunt Margaret was seated; her gray lavender dress was carefully spread about her, her white hair turned back beneath a black velvet satin-lined hood, and a lace fichu pinned across her breast.

"You here, Miss Vine?"

"Yes; and I thought I would save you a thankless effort. You could not overtake the girls unless you ran."

"I was not going to try and overtake them, Miss Vine," said Leslie coldly.

"Indeed! I beg your pardon; I thought you were. But would you mind, Mr. Leslie —it is a very trifling request, but I set store by these little relics of our early history— Miss *Marguerite* Vine, if you would be so kind?"

Leslie bowed. "Certainly, Miss Marguerite," he said quietly.

"Thank you," she said, detaining him. "It is very good of you. Of course you are surprised to see me up here?"

"Oh no," said Leslie quietly. "It is a delightful place to sit and rest and read."

"Ye—es; but I cannot say that I care much for the rough walking of this part of the world, and my brother seems somehow to have taken quite a dislike to the idea of having a carriage?"

"Yes?"

"So I am obliged to walk when I do come out. There are certain duties one is forced to attend to. For instance, there is my poor brother up yonder. I feel bound to see him from time to time. You see him frequently, of course ? "

"Every day, necessarily. We are so near."

" Poor fellow! yes. Very eccentric and peculiar; but you need be under no apprehension, Mr. Leslie. He is quite harmless, I am sure."

"Oh, quite harmless, Miss Marguerite. Merely original."

" It is very good of you to call it originality; but as friends, Mr. Leslie, there is no harm in our alluding to his poor brain. Softening, a medical man told me."

" Hardening, I should say," thought Leslie.

" Very peculiar ! very peculiar ! Father and uncle both so different from my dear nephew. He is in very bad spirits. Ah ! Mr. Leslie, I shall be very glad to see him once more as a Des Vignes should be. With him placed in the position that should be his, and that engagement carried out regarding my darling Louise's future, I could leave this world of sorrow without a sigh."

Leslie winced, but it was not perceptible to

Aunt Marguerite, who, feeling dissatisfied with the result of her shot, fired again.

"Of course it would involve losing my darling; but at my time of life, Mr. Leslie, one has learned that it is one's duty always to study self-sacrifice. The Des Vignes were always a self-sacrificing family. When it was not for some one or other of their kindred it was for their king, and then for their faith. You know our old French motto, Mr. Leslie?"

"I? No. I beg pardon."

"Really? I should have thought that you could not fail to see that. It is almost the only trace of our former greatness that my misguided brother——"

"Were you alluding to Mr. Luke Vine?"

"No, no, no, no! To my brother, George des Vignes. Surely, Mr. Leslie, you must have noted our arms upon the dining-room windows."

"Oh, yes, of course, of course; and the motto, *Roy et Foy*."

"Exactly," said Aunt Marguerite, smiling. "I thought it must have caught your eye."

Something else was catching Duncan Leslie's eye just then—the last flutter of the scarf Louise wore before it disappeared round the foot of the cliff.

" I shall bear it, I dare say, and with for-
titude, Mr. Leslie, for it will be a grand
position that she will take. The De Lignys
are a family almost as old as our own ; and
fate might arrange for me to visit them and
make a long stay. She's a sweet girl, is she
not, Mr. Leslie ? "

" Miss Vine ?  Yes ; you must be very
proud of her," said the young man, without
moving a muscle.

" We are ; we are indeed, Mr. Leslie ; but I
am afraid I am detaining you."

" It is curious," said Leslie, as he walked
slowly down the cliff-path.  " De Ligny, De
Ligny ?  Who is De Ligny ?  Well," he added
with a sigh, " I ought to thank Heaven that
the name is not Pradelle."

# CHAPTER IX.

## IN OFFICE HOURS.

"Now, my dear Mr. Crampton, believe me, I am only actuated by a desire to do good."

"That's exactly what actuates me, sir, when I make bold, after forty years' service with you and your father, to tell you that you have made a great mistake."

"All men make mistakes, Crampton," said Van Heldre to his plump, gray, stern-looking head clerk.

"Yes, sir, but if they are then worth their salt they see where they have made a mistake, and try and correct it. We did not want him."

"As far as actual work to be done, no; but I will tell you plainly why I took on the young man. I wish to help my old friend in a peculiarly troubled period of his life."

"That's you all over, Mr. Van Heldre," said the old clerk, pinching his very red nose, and then arranging his thin hair with a pen-holder, "but I can't feel that it's right. You see, the young man don't take to his work. He comes and goes in a supercilious manner, and treats me as if I were his servant."

"Oh, that will soon pass off, Crampton."

"I hope so, Mr. Van Heldre, sir, but his writing's as bad as a schoolboy's."

"That will improve."

"He's always late of a morning."

"I'll ask him to correct that."

"And he's always doing what I hate in a young man, seeing how short is life, sir, and how soon we're gone—he's always looking at the clock and yawning."

"Never mind, Crampton, he'll soon give up all that sort of thing. The young man is like an ill-trained tree. He has grown rather wild, but now he has been transplanted to an orderly office, to be under your constant supervision, he will gradually imbibe your habits and precision. It will be his making."

"Now, now, now," said the old clerk, shaking his head, "that's flattering, sir. My habits and precision. No, no, sir; I'm a very bad clerk, and I'm growing old as fast as I can."

"You are the best clerk in the west of England, Crampton, and you are only growing old at the customary rate. And now to oblige me look over these little blemishes in the young man's character. There is a good deal of the spoiled boy in him, but I believe his heart's right; and for more reasons than one I want him to develop into a good man of business—such a one as we can make of him if we try."

"Don't say another word, Mr. Van Heldre. You know me, and if I say as long as the young man is honest and straightforward I'll do my best for him, I suppose that's sufficient."

"More than sufficient, Crampton."

"But you know, sir, he ought to have made some little advance in a month."

"No, no, Crampton," said Van Heldre, smiling, "he has not grown used to the new suit yet; have patience, and he'll come right."

"That's enough, sir," said Crampton, climbing on to a high stool in front of a well-polished desk; "now for business. The *St. Aubyn* has taken in all her cargo, and will sail to-morrow. We ought soon to have news of the *Madelaine*. By the way, I hope Miss Madelaine's quite well, sir. Haven't seen her for a day and a half."

"Quite well, Crampton."

"That's right, sir," said the old man, smiling, and rubbing his hands. "Bless her! I've only one thing against her. Why wasn't she a boy?"

Van Heldre smiled at his old confidential man, who still rubbed his hands softly, and gazed over his silver-rimmed spectacles at a file of bills of lading hanging from the wall.

"What a boy she would have made, and what a man I could have made of him! Van Heldre and Son once more, as it ought to be. I'd have made just such a man of business of him as I made of you. Going, sir?"

"Yes, I'm going up to Tolzarn. By the way, send Mr. Henry Vine up to me about twelve."

"Yes, sir," said Crampton, beginning to write away very busily. "I suppose he'll come?"

"Of course, of course," said Van Heldre, hastily, and leaving the office he went into the morning-room, where Madelaine was busy with her needle.

She looked at him in an inquiring way, to

which he had become accustomed during the past month, and in accordance with an unwritten contract.

" No, my dear, not come yet."

Madelaine's countenance changed as she saw her father glance at his watch, and she involuntarily darted a quick look at the clock on the chimney-piece.

" I'm going up to the works," continued Van Heldre. " Back before one. Morning."

Madelaine resumed her work for a few minutes, and then rose to stand where, unseen, she could watch the road. She saw her father go by up the valley, but her attention was turned toward the sea, from which direction Harry Vine would have to come.

She stood watching for nearly a quarter of an hour before she heard a familiar step, and then the young man passed smoking the end of a cigar, which he threw away before turning in at the way which led to Van Heldre's offices.

Directly after, as Madelaine sat looking very thoughtful over her work, there was the quick patter of Mrs. Van Heldre's feet.

" Madelaine, my dear," she said as she entered, " I thought you said that Mr. Pradelle had gone away a fortnight ago."

" I did, mamma."

" Well, then, he has come back again."

" Back again ? "

" Yes, I was at the up-stairs window just now and I saw him pass as I was looking out for Harry Vine. He's very late this morning, and it does make papa so vexed."

It was late, for instead of being nine o'clock, the clock in the office was on the stroke of ten as Harry Vine hurriedly entered, and glanced at the yellowy-white faced dial.

" Morning, Mr. Crampton. I say, that clock's fast, isn't it ? "

" Eh ? fast ? " said the old man grimly. " No, Mr. Harry Vine ; that's a steady old time-keeper, not a modern young man."

" Disagreeable old hunks," said Harry to himself, as he hung up his hat. " Bad head-ache this morning, Mr. Crampton, thought I shouldn't be able to come."

" Seidlitz powder," said the old man, scratching away with his pen.

" Eh ? "

" Dissolve the blue in a tumbler of warm water."

" Bother ! " muttered Harry, frowning.

" The white in a wineglassful of cold.

Pour one into the other—and—drink—while effervescing."

The intervals between some of the words were filled up by scratches of the pen.

" Headache, eh ? Bad things, sir, bad things."

He removed himself from his stool and went to the safe in the inner office, where Van Heldre generally sat, and Harry raised his head from his desk and listened, as he heard the rattling of keys and the clang of a small iron door.

" Yes, bad things headaches, Mr. Harry," said the old man returning. " Try early hours for 'em ; and look here, Mr. Van Heldre says——"

" Has he been in the office this morning ? "

" Yes, sir, he came in as soon as I'd come, nine to the minute, and he wants you to join him at the tin works about twelve."

" Wigging ! " said guilty conscience.

" Do your head good, sir."

Old Crampton resumed his seat, and for an hour and three quarters, during which period Harry had several times looked at the clock and yawned, there was a constant scratching of pens.

Then Harry Vine descended from his stool.

"I'd better go now?"

"Yes, sir, you'd better go now. And might have gone before for all the good you've done," grumbled the old man, as Harry passed the window.

The old man had hardly spent another half-hour over his work when there was a sharp tapping at the door, such as might be given by the knob on a stick.

"Come in."

The door was opened, and Pradelle entered and gave a sharp look round.

"Morning," he said in a cavalier way. "Tell Mr. Vine I want to speak to him for a moment."

Old Crampton looked up from his writing, and fixed his eyes on the visitor's hat.

"Not at home," he said shortly.

"How long will he be?"

"Don't know."

"Where has he gone?"

"Tin works."

"Confounded old bear!" muttered Pradelle as he went out, after frowning severely at the old clerk, who did not see it.

"Idle young puppy!" grumbled Crampton, dotting an *i* so fiercely that he drove his pen through the paper. "I'd have knocked his hat off if I had had my ruler handy."

Van Heldre was busy at work with a shovel when Harry Vine reached the tin-smelting works, which the merchant had added to his other ventures. He was beside a heap of what rather resembled wet coarsely ground coffee.

"Ah, Harry," he said, "you may as well learn all these things. Be useful some day. Take hold of that shovel and turn that over."

A strong mind generally acts upon one that is weak, and it was so here.

Harry felt disposed, as he looked at his white hands, the shovel, and the heap, to thrust the said white hands into his pockets and walk away.

But he took the shovel and plunged it in the heap, lifted it full, and then with a look of disgust said—

"What am I to do with it ?"

"Shovel it away and get more out of the centre."

Harry obeyed, and looked up.

"Now take a couple of handfuls and examine them. Don't be afraid, man, it's honest dirt."

Van Heldre set the example, took a handful, and poured it from left to right and back.

"Now," he said, "take notice : that's badly washed."

"Not soap enough," said Harry, hiding his annoyance with an attempt at being facetious.

"Not exactly," said Van Heldre dryly; "bad work. Now when that tin is passed through the furnace there'll be twice as much slag and refuse as there ought to be. That will do. Leave the shovel, I want you to take account of those slabs of tin. Mark them, number them, and enter them in this book. It will take you an hour. Then bring the account down to me at the office."

"I can have a man to move the slabs ?"

"No : they are all busy. If I were doing it, I should work without a man."

"Hang it all! I'm about sick of this," said Harry. "How mad Aunt Marguerite would be if she could see me now!"

He looked round at the low dirty sheds on one side, at the row of furnaces on the other, two of which emitted a steady roar as the tin within gradually turned from a brown granulated powder to a golden fluid, whose stony scum was floating on the top.

"It's enough to make any man kick against his fate. Nice occupation for a gentleman, 'pon my word!"

A low whistle made him look up.

"Why, Vic," he cried; "I thought you were in town."

"How are you, my Trojan?" cried the visitor boisterously. "I was in town, but I've come back. I say, cheerful work this for Monsieur le Comte Henri des Vignes!"

"Don't chaff a fellow," said Harry angrily. "What brought you down?"

"Two things."

"Now, look here, Vic. Don't say any more about that. Perhaps after a time I may get her to think differently, but now——"

"I was not going to say anything about your sister, my dear boy. I can wait and bear anything. But I suppose I may say something about you."

"About me?"

"Yes. I've got a splendid thing on. Safe to make money—heaps of it."

"Yes; but your schemes always want money first."

"Well, hang it all, lad! you can't expect a crop of potatoes without planting a few bits first. It wouldn't want much. Only about fifty pounds. A hundred would be better, but we could make fifty do."

Harry shook his head.

"Come, come; you haven't heard half yet. I've the genuine information. It would be worth a pile of money. It's our chance now —such a chance as may never occur again."

"No, no; don't tempt me, Vic," said Harry, after a long whispered conversation.

"Tempt? I feel disposed to force you, lad. It makes me half wild to see you degraded to such work as this. Why, if we do as I propose, you will be in a position to follow out your aunt's instructions, engage lawyers to push on your case, and while you obtain your rights, I shall be in a position to ask your sister's hand without the chance of a refusal. I tell you the thing's safe."

"No, no," said Harry, shaking his head; "it's too risky. We should lose and be worse off than ever."

"With a horse like that, and me with safe private information about him!"

"No," said Harry, "I won't. I'm going to keep steadily on here, and, as the governor calls it, plod."

"That you're not, if I know it," cried Pradelle, indignantly. "I won't stand it.

It's disgraceful. You shan't throw yourself away."

"But I've got no money, old fellow."

"Nonsense! Get some of the old man."

"No; I've done it too often. He won't stand it now."

"Well, of your aunt."

"She hasn't a penny but what my father lets her have."

"Your sister. Come, she would let you have some."

Harry shook his head.

"No, I'm not going to ask her. It's no good, Vic; I won't."

"Well," said Pradelle, apostrophizing an ingot of tin as it lay at his feet glistening with iridescent hues, "if any one had told me, I wouldn't have believed it. Why, Harry, lad, you've only been a month at this mill-horse life, and you're quite changed. What have they been doing to you, man?"

"Breaking my spirit, I suppose they'd call it," said the young man bitterly.

Harry shook his head.

"Get out! I won't have it. You want waking up," said Pradelle, in a low, earnest voice. "Think, lad, a few pounds placed as I could place 'em, and there's fortune for us both, without reckoning on what you could do in France. As your aunt says, there's money and a title waiting for you, if you'll only stretch out your hand to take 'em. Come, rouse yourself. Harry Vine isn't the lad to settle down to this drudgery. Why, I thought it was one of the workmen when I came up."

"It's of no use," said Harry gloomily, as he seated himself on the ingots of tin. "A man must submit to his fate."

"Bah! a man's fate is what he makes it. Look here; fifty or a hundred borrowed for a few days, and then repaid."

"But suppose——"

"Suppose!" cried Pradelle mockingly; "a business man has no time to suppose. He strikes while the iron's hot. You're going to strike iron, not tin."

"How? Where's the money?"

"Where's the money?" said Pradelle mockingly. "You wan't fifty or a hundred for a few days, when you could return it fifty times over; and you say, where's the money?"

"Don't I tell you I have no one I could borrow from?" said Harry angrily.

"Yes, you have," said Pradelle, sinking his

voice. "It's easy as easy. Only for a few days. A temporary loan. Look here."

He bent down, and whispered a few words in the young man's ear, words which turned him crimson, and then deadly pale.

"Pradelle!" he cried, in a hoarse whisper; "are you mad?"

"No. I was thinking of coming over to Auvergne to spend a month with my friend, the Count. By and by, dear lad—by and by."

"No, no; it is impossible," said Harry, hoarsely, and he gave a hasty glance round. "I couldn't do that."

"You could," said Pradelle, and then to himself; "and, if I know you, Harry Vine, you shall."

# CHAPTER X.

BREAKFAST-TIME, with George Vine quietly partaking of his toast and giving furtive glances at a *Beloe* in a small squat bottle. He was feeding his mind at the same time that he supplied the wants of his body. Now it was a bite of toast, leaving in the embrowned bread such a mark as was seen by the dervish when the man asked after the lost camel; for the student of molluscous sea-life had lost a front tooth. Now it was a glance at the little gooseberry-shaped creature, clear as crystal, glistening in the clear water with iridescent hues, and trailing behind it a couple of filaments of an extreme delicacy and beauty that warranted the student's admiration.

Louise was seated opposite, performing matutinal experiments, so it seemed, with pots, cups, an urn, and various infusions and crystals.

Pradelle was reading the paper, and Harry was dividing his time between eating some fried ham and glancing at the clock, which was pointing in the direction of the hour when he should be at Van Heldre's.

"More tea, Louie; too sweet," said the head of the house, passing his cup, *viâ* Pradelle.

The cup was filled up and passed back, Louise failing to notice that Pradelle manœuvred to touch her hand as he played his part in the transfer. Then the door opened, and Liza, the brown-faced, black-haired Cornish maid, entered, bearing a tray with an untouched cup of tea, a brown piece of ham on its plate, and a little covered dish of hot toast.

"Please, 'm, Miss Vine says she don't want no breakfast this morning."

The *Beloe* bottle dropped back into George Vine's pocket.

"Eh? My sister ill?" he said anxiously.

"No, sir; she seems quite well, but she was gashly cross with me, and said why didn't Miss Louie bring it up."

"Liza, I forbad you to use that foolish word, 'gashly,'" said Louise, pouring out a fresh cup of tea, and changing it for the one cooling on the tray.

"Why don't you take up auntie's breakfast as you always do? You know she doesn't like it sent up."

Louise made no reply to her brother, but turned to Pradelle.

"You will excuse me for a few minutes, Mr. Pradelle," she said, as she rose.

"Excuse—you?" he replied, with a peculiar smile; and, rising in turn, he managed so badly as he hurried to the door to open it for Louise's passage with the tray, that he and Liza, bent on the same errand, came into collision.

"Thank you, Mr. Pradelle," said Louise, quietly, as she passed out with the tray, and Liza gave him an indignant glance as she closed the door.

"Ha, ha! What a bungle!" cried Harry mockingly, as he helped himself to more ham.

George Vine was absorbed once more in the study of the *Beloe*.

"Never you mind, my lord the count," said Pradelle in an undertone; "I don't see that you get on so very well."

Harry winced.

"What are you going to do this morning?"

"Fish."

"Humph! well to be you," said Harry, with

a vicious bite at his bread, while his father was too much absorbed in his study even to hear. "You're going loafing about, and I've got to go and turn that grindstone."

"Which you can leave whenever you like," said Pradelle meaningly.

"Hold your tongue!" cried Harry roughly, as the door re-opened, and Louise, looking slightly flushed, again took her place at the table.

"Aunt poorly?" said Vine.

"Oh, no, papa; she is having her breakfast now."

"If you're too idle to take up auntie's breakfast, I'll take it," said Harry severely. "Don't send it up by that girl again."

"I shall always take it myself, Harry," said Louise quietly.

The breakfast was ended; George Vine went to his study to feed his sea-anemones on chopped whelk; Pradelle made an excuse about fishing lines, after reading plainly enough that his presence was unwelcome; and Harry stood with his hands in his pockets, looking on as his sister put away the tea-caddy.

"Will you not be late, Harry?"

"Perhaps," he said, ill-humouredly. "I

shall be there as soon as old bottle-nose I dare say."

"How long is Mr. Pradelle going to stay?"

" Long as I like."

There was a pause. Then Harry continued. " He's a friend of mine, a gentleman, and Aunt Marguerite likes him to stay."

"Yes," said Louise gravely. "Aunt Marguerite seems to like him."

" And so do you, only you're such a precious coquette."

Louise raised her eyebrows. This was news to her, but she said nothing.

"The more any one sees of Pradelle the more one likes him. Deal nicer fellow than that Scotch prig Leslie."

There was a slight flush on Louise Vine's face, but she did not speak, merely glanced at the clock.

"All right ; I'm not going yet."

Then, changing his manner—

" Oh, Lou, you can't think what a life it is," he cried impetuously.

" Why, Harry, it ought to be a very pleasant one."

" What, with your nose over an account book, and every time you happen to look up, old Crampton staring at you as much as to say, ' Why don't you go on ? ' "

" Never mind, dear. Try and think that it is for your good."

" For my good ! " he said with a mocking laugh.

" Yes, and to please father. Why, Harry dear, is it not something to have a chance to redeem your character ? "

" Redeem my grandmother ! I've never lost it. Why, Lou, it's too bad. Here's father rich as a Jew, and Uncle Luke with no end of money."

" Has he, Harry ? " said Louise thoughtfully. " Really I don't know."

" I'm sure he has—lots. A jolly old miser, and no one to leave it to ; and I don't see then why I should be ground down to work like an errand-boy."

" Don't make a sentimental grievance of it, dear, but go and do your duty like a man."

" If I do my duty like a man I shall go and try to recover the French estates which my father neglects."

" No, don't do that, dear ; go and get my old school spelling-book and read the fable of the dog and the shadow."

" There you go, sneering again. You

women can't understand a fellow. Here am
I worried to death for money, and have to
drudge as old Van Heldre's clerk."

" Worried for money, Harry? What nonsense!"

"I am. You don't know. I say, Lou dear."

" Now, Harry! you will be so late."

" I won't go at all if you don't listen to me.
Look here; I want fifty pounds."

" What for?"

" Never mind. Will you lend it to me?"

" But what can you want with fifty pounds,
Harry? You're not in debt?"

" You've got some saved up. Now, lend it
to me, there's a good girl; I'll pay you again,
honour bright."

" Harry, I've lent you money till I'm tired
of lending, and you never do pay me back."

" But I will this time."

Louise shook her head.

" What, you don't believe me?"

" I believe you would pay me again if you
had the money; but if I lent it you would
spend it, and be as poor as ever in a month."

" Not this time, Lou. Lend it to me."

She shook her head.

" Then hang me if I don't go and ask
Duncan Leslie."

"Harry! No; you would not degrade yourself to that."

"Will you lend it?"

"No."

"Then I will ask him. The poor fool will think it will please you, and lend it directly. I'll make it a hundred whilst I'm about it."

"Harry!"

"Too late now," he cried, and he hurried away.

"Oh!" ejaculated Louise, as she stood gazing after him with her cheeks burning. "No," she said, after a pause; "it was only a threat; he would not dare."

"Harry gone to his office?" said Vine, entering the room.

"Yes, dear."

"Mr. Pradelle gone too?"

"Yes, dear; fishing, I think."

"Hum. Makes this house quite his home."

"Yes, papa; and do you think we are doing right?"

"Eh?" said Vine sharply, as he dragged his mind back from where it had gone under a tide-covered rock. "Oh, I see, about having that young man here. Well, Louie, it's like this: I don't want to draw the rein too tightly. Harry is at work now, and keeping to it.

Van Heldre says his conduct is very fair.
Harry likes Mr. Pradelle, and they are old
companions, so I feel disposed to wink at
the intimacy, so long as our boy keeps to
his business."

"Perhaps you are right, dear," said Louise.

"You don't like Mr. Pradelle, my dear?"

"No, I do not."

"No fear of his robbing me of you, eh?"

"Oh, father!"

"That's right; that's right; and look here,
as we're talking about that little thing which
makes the world go round, please understand
this, and help me, my dear. There's to be no
nonsense between Harry and Madelaine."

"Then you don't like Madelaine?"

"Eh? What? Not like her? Bless her!
You've almost cause to be jealous, only you
need not be, for I've room in my heart for
both of you. I love her too well to let her
be made uncomfortable by our family scapegrace. Dear me! I'm sure that it has."

"Have you lost anything, dear?"

"Yes, a glass stopper. Perhaps I left it
in my room. Mustn't lose it; stoppers cost
money."

"And here's some money of yours, father."

"Eh? Oh, that change."

"Twenty-five shillings."

"Put it on the chimney-piece, my dear; I'll take it presently. We will not be hard on Harry. Let him have his companion. We shall get him round by degrees. Ah, here comes some one to tempt you away."

In effect Madelaine was passing the window on her way to the front entrance; but Vine forgot all about his glass stopper for the moment, and threw open the glass door.

"Come in here, my dear," he said. "We were just talking about you."

"About me, Mr. Vine? Whatever were you saying?"

"Slander of course, of course."

"My father desired to be kindly remembered, and I was to say, 'Very satisfactory so far.'"

"Very satisfactory so far?" said Vine dreamily.

"He said you would know what it meant."

"To be sure—to be sure. Louie, my dear, I'm afraid your aunt is right. My brain is getting to be like that of a jelly-fish."

He nodded laughingly and left the room.

"Did you meet Harry as you came?" said Louise, as soon as they were alone.

"Yes; but he kept on one side of the street, and I was on the other."

"Didn't he cross over to speak?"

"No; he couldn't see the Dutch fraulein—the Dutch doll."

"Oh, that's cruel, Maddy. I did not think my aunt's words could sting you."

"Well, sometimes I don't think they do, but at others they seem to rankle. But look, isn't that Mr. Pradelle coming?"

For answer Louise caught her friend's hand to hurry her out of the room before Pradelle entered.

# CHAPTER XI.

THAT morning after breakfast Aunt Marguerite sat by her open window in her old-fashioned French *peignoir*.

She saw Pradelle go out, and she smiled and beamed as he turned to look up at her window, and raised his hat before proceeding down into the back lanes of the port to inveigle an urchin into the task of obtaining for him a pot of ragworms for bait.

Soon after she saw her nephew go out, but he did not raise his head. On the contrary, he bent it down, and heaved up his shoulders like a wet sailor, as he went on to his office.

"*Mon pauvre enfant!*" she murmured, as she half closed her eyes, and kissed the tips of her fingers. "But wait a while, Henri, *mon enfant*, and all shall be well."

There was a lapse of time devoted to thought, and then Aunt Marguerite's eyes glistened with malice, as she saw Madelaine approach.

"Pah !" she ejaculated softly. "This might be Amsterdam or the Boompjes. Wretched Dutch wench ! How can George tolerate her presence here !"

Then Pradelle came back, but he did not look up this time, merely went to the door and entered, his eyes looking searchingly about as if in search of Louise.

Lastly, a couple of particularly unseamanlike men, dressed in shiny tarpaulin hats and pea-jackets, with earrings and very smooth pomatumy hair, came into sight. Each man carried a pack and a big stick, and as they drew near their eyes wandered over window and door in a particularly searching way.

They did not come to the front, but in a slouching, furtive way went past the front of the house and round to the back, where the next minute there was a low tapping made by the knob of a stick on a door, and soon after a buzzing murmur of voices arose.

Aunt Marguerite had nothing whatever to do, and the murmur interested her to the extent of making her rise, go across her room, and through a door at the back into her bedchamber, where an open lattice window had a chair beneath, and the said window being just over the back entrance from whence the murmur came, Aunt Marguerite had nothing to do but go and sit down there unseen, and hear every word that was said.

"Yes," said the familiar voice of brown-faced, black-haired Liza; "they're beautiful, but I haven't got the money."

"That there red ribbon 'd just soot you, my lass," said a deep voice, so fuzzy that it must have come from under a woollen jacket.

"Just look at that there hankychy, too," said another deep voice. "Did you ever see a better match?"

"Never," said the other deep voice emphatically.

"Yes, they're very lovely, but I ain't got the money. I let mother have all I had this week."

"Never mind the gashly money, my lass," said the first deep-voiced man huskily, "ain't-cher got nothing you can sell?"

Then arose a good deal of murmuring whisper, and Aunt Marguerite's lips became like a pale pink line drawn across the lower part of her face, and both her eyes were closely shut.

"Well, you wait," was the concluding

sentence of the whispered trio, and then the door was heard to shut.

The click of a latch rose to where Aunt Marguerite sat, and then there was a trio once again—a whispered trio—ending with a little rustling, and the sound of heavy steps.

Then the door closed, and Liza, daughter of Poll Perrow, the fishwoman, who carried a heavy maund by the help of a strap across her forehead, hurried up to her bedroom, and threw herself upon her knees as she spread two or three yards of brilliant red ribbon on the bed, and tastefully placed beside the ribbon an orange silk kerchief, whose united colours made her dark eyes sparkle with delight.

The quick ringing of a bell put an end to the colour-worship, and Liza, with a hasty ejaculation, opened her box, thrust in her new treasures, dropped the lid, and locked it again before hurrying down to the dining-room, where she found her young mistress, her master, and Madelaine Van Heldre.

"There was some change on the chimney-piece, Liza," said Louise. "Did you see it?"

"No, miss."

"It is very strange. You are quite sure you did not take it, papa?"

" Quite, my dear."

" That will do, Liza."

The girl went out, looking scared.

" It is very strange," said Vine.

" Yes, dear; and it is a great trouble to me. This is the third time money has been missing lately. I don't like to suspect people, but one seems to be forced."

" But surely, Louie, dear, that poor girl would not take it."

" I have always tried to hope not, Maddy," said Louise sadly.

" You had better make a change."

" Send her away, father? How can I do that? How can I recommend her for another situation ? "

" Ah! it's a puzzle—it's a puzzle," said Vine irritably. " One of the great difficulties of domestic service. I shall soon begin to think that your Uncle Luke is right after all. He has no troubles, eh, Louise ? "

She looked up in his face with a peculiar smile, but made no reply. Her father, however, seemed to read her look, and continued,

" Ah, well, I dare say you are right, my dear; we can't get away from trouble; and if we don't have one kind we have another.

Get more than our share, though, in this house."

Louise smiled in his face, and the comical aspect of chagrin displayed resulted in a general laugh.

" Is one of the sea-anemones dead ? "

" Yes, confound it ! and it has poisoned the water, so that I am afraid the rest will go."

" I think we can get over that trouble," said Louise, laughing. " It will be an excuse for a pleasant ramble with you."

" Yes," said Vine dryly, " but we shall not get over the trouble of the thief quite so well. I'm afraid these Perrows are a dishonest family. I'll speak to the girl."

" No, father, leave it to me."

" Very well, my child ; but I think you ought to speak."

The old man left the room, the bell was rung, and Liza summoned, when a scene of tears and protestations arose, resulting in a passionate declaration that Liza would tell her mother, that she would not stop in a house where she was going to be suspected, and that she had never taken anybody's money but her own.

" This is the third time that I have missed money, Liza, or I would not have spoken. If you took it, confess like a good girl, and we'll forgive you if you promise never to take anything of the kind again."

" I can't confess, miss, and won't confess," sobbed the girl.   " Mother shall come and speak to you.   I wouldn't do such a thing."

" Where did you get the money with which you bought the red ribbon and orange kerchief this morning, Liza?" said a voice at the door.

All started to see that Aunt Marguerite was there looking on, and apparently the recipient of all that had been said.

Liza stood with eyes dilated, and jaw dropped.

" Then you've been at my box," she suddenly exclaimed.   " Ah, what a shame!"

" At your box, you wretched creature!" said Aunt Marguerite contemptuously.   " Do you suppose I should go into your room?"

" You've been opening my box," said the girl again, more angrily; " and it's a shame."

" I saw her take them up to her room, Louise.   My dear, she was buying them under my window, of some pedlar.   You had better send her away."

Liza did not wait to be sent away from the room, but ran out sobbing, to hurry up-stairs to her bed-chamber, open her box, and see if the brilliant specimens of silken fabric were safe, and then cry over them till they were blotched with her tears.

"A bad family," said Aunt Marguerite. "I'm quite sure that girl stole my piece of muslin lace, and gave it to that wretched woman your Uncle Luke encourages."

"No, no, aunt, you lost that piece of lace one day when you were out."

"Nonsense, child! your memory is not good.   Who is that with you?   Oh, I see; Miss Van Heldre."

Aunt Marguerite, after suddenly becoming aware of the presence of Madelaine, made a most ceremonious curtsy, and then sailed out of the room.

"Louise must be forced to give up the companionship of that wretched Dutch girl," she said as she reached her own door, at which she paused to listen to Liza sobbing.

"I wonder what Miss Vine would have been like," thought Madelaine, "if she had married some good sensible man, and had a large family to well employ her mind?" Then she asked herself what kind of man she would have selected as possessing the necessary qualifications, and concluded that he should have been such a man as Duncan

Leslie, and wondered whether he would marry her friend.

" Why, Madelaine," said Louise, breaking her chain of thought, " what are you thinking about ? "

" Thinking about ? " said the girl, starting, and colouring slightly. " Oh, I was thinking about Mr. Leslie just then."

# CHAPTER XII

" LATE again," said old Crampton, as Harry Vine entered the office.

" How I do hate the sight of that man's nose ! " said the young man; and he stared hard, as if forced by some attraction.

The old clerk frowned, and felt annoyed.

. " I beg pardon," he said.

" Granted," said Harry, coolly.

" I said I beg pardon, Mr. Harry Vine."

" I heard you."

" But I thought you spoke."

" No," grumbled Harry; " didn't speak."

" Then I will," said old Crampton merrily. " Good morning, Mr. Harry Vine," and he rattled the big ruler by his desk.

" Eh? oh, yes, I see. Didn't say it as I came in. Good morning, Mr. Crampton."

" Lesson for the proud young upstart in good behaviour," grumbled old Crampton.

"Bother him!" muttered Harry, as he took his place at his desk, opened a big account book Crampton placed before him, with some amounts to transfer from one that was smaller, and began writing.

But as he wrote, the figures seemed to join hands and dance before him; then his pen ceased to form others, and an imaginary picture painted itself on the·delicately tinted blue paper with its red lines—a pleasant land-scape in fair France with sunny hill-sides on which ranged in rows were carefully cultured vines. To the north and east were softened bosky woods, and dominating all, one of those antique castellated chateaus, with pepper-box towers and gilded vanes, such as he had seen in pictures or read of in some books.

"If I only had the money," thought Harry, as he entered a sum similar to that which Pradelle had named. "He knows all these things. He has good advice from friends, and if we won—Hah!"

The chateau rose before his eyes again, bathed in sunshine. Then he pictured the terrace overlooking the vineyards—a gray old stone terrace, with many seats and sheltering trees, and along that terrace walked just such a maiden as Aunt Marguerite had described.

*Scratch! scratch! scratch! scratch!* His
pen and Crampton's pen; and he had no
money, and Pradelle's project to borrow as
he had suggested was absurd.

Ah, if he only had eighty-one pounds ten
shillings and sixpence! the sum he now placed
in neat figures in their appropriate columns.

Old Crampton tilted back his tall stool,
swung himself round, and lowered himself
to the ground. Then crossing the office, he
went into Van Heldre's private room, and
there was the rattle of a key, a creaking
hinge, as an iron door was swung open; and
directly after the old man returned.

Harry Vine could not see his hands, and he
did not raise his eyes to watch the old clerk,
but in the imagination which so readily
pictured the chateau that was not in Spain,
he seemed to see as he heard every movement
of the fat, white fingers, when a canvas bag
was dumped down on the mahogany desk, the
string untied, and a little heap of coins were
poured out. Then followed the scratching of
those coins upon the mahogany, as they were
counted, ranged in little piles, and finally,
after an entry had been checked, they were
replaced in the bag, which the old man bore
back into the safe in the private room.

"Fifty or a hundred pounds," said Harry to himself, as a curious sensation of heat came into his cheeks, to balance which there seemed to be a peculiarly cold thrill running up his spine, to the nape of his neck.

"Anybody at home?"

"Yes, sir; here we are, hard at work."

Harry had looked up sharply to see Uncle Luke standing in the opening, a grim-looking gray figure in his old Norfolk jacket and straw hat, one hand resting on his heavy stick, the other carrying a battered fish-basket. The old man's face was in shadow, for the sunshine streamed in behind him, but there was plenty of light to display his grim, sardonic features, as, after a short nod to Crampton, he gazed from under his shaggy brows piercingly at his nephew.

"Well, quill-driver," he said, sneeringly; "doing something useful at last?"

"Morning, uncle," said Harry shortly; and he muttered to himself, "I should like to throw the ledger at him."

"Hope he's a good boy, hey?"

"Oh, he's getting on, Mr. Luke Vine—slowly," said Crampton unwillingly. "He'll do better by and by."

A sharp remark was on Harry's lips, but

he checked it for a particular reason. Uncle
Luke might have the money he wanted.

"Time he did," said the old man. "Look
here, boy," he continued, with galling, sneering tone in his voice. "Go and tell your
master I want to see him."

Harry drew a long breath, and his teeth
gritted together.

"I caught a splendid conger this morning,"
continued Uncle Luke, giving his basket a
swing, "and I've brought your master half."

"My master!" muttered Harry.

"Like conger-pie, boy?"

"No," said Harry, shortly.

"More nice than wise," said Uncle Luke.
"Always were. There, be quick. I want to
see your master."

"To see my master," thought Harry, with a
strange feeling of exasperation in his breast as
he looked up at Crampton.

Crampton was looking up at him with eyes
which said very clearly, "Well, why don't you
go?"

"They'll make me an errand-boy next," said
the young man to himself, as, after twisting
his locket round and round like a firework, he
swung himself down, "and want me to clean
the knives and boots and shoes."

"Tell him I'm in a hurry," said Uncle Luke, as Harry reached the door which led into the private house along a passage built and covered with glass, by one side of what was originally a garden.

"Ah," said Uncle Luke, going closer to old Crampton's desk, and taking down from where it rested on two brass hooks, the heavy ebony ruler. "Nice bit o' wood that."

"Yes, sir," said the old clerk, in the fidgety way of a workman who objects to have his tools touched.

"Pretty weighty," continued Uncle Luke, balancing it in his hand. "Give a man a pretty good topper that, eh?"

"Yes, Mr. Luke Vine.—I should like to give him one with it," thought Crampton.

"Do for a constable's staff, or to kill burglars, eh?"

"Capitally, sir."

"Hah! You don't get burglars here, though, do you?"

"No, sir; never had any yet."

"Good job too," said Uncle Luke, putting the ruler back in its place, greatly to Crampton's relief. "Rather an awkward cub to lick into shape, my nephew, eh?"

"Rather, sir."

" Well, you must lick away, Crampton—not with that ruler though," he chuckled. " Time something was made of him—not a bad sort of boy; but spoiled."

" I shall do my best, Mr. Luke Vine," said Crampton dryly; " but I must tell you candidly, sir, he's too much of the gentleman for us, and he feels it."

" Bah !"

" Not at all the sort of young man I should have selected for a clerk."

" Never mind; make the best of him."

" Mr. Van Heldre is coming, sir," said Harry coldly, as he re-entered the office.

" Bah ! I didn't tell you to bring him here. I want to go in there."

As Luke Vine spoke, he rose and moved to the door.

" Be a good boy," he said, turning with a peculiar smile at his nephew. " I dare say you'll get on."

" Oh !" muttered Harry, as he retook his place at his desk, " how I should like to tell you, Uncle Luke, just what I think."

The door closed behind the old man, who had nearly reached the end of the long passage, when he met Van Heldre.

" Ah, Luke Vine, I was just coming."

"Go back," said the visitor, making a stab at the merchant with his stick. " Brought you something. Where's Mrs. Van Heldre ?"

" In the breakfast-room. Come along."

Van Heldre clapped the old man on the shoulder, and led him into the room where Mrs. Van Heldre was seated at work.

"Ah, Mr. Luke Vine," she cried, "who'd have thought of seeing you ?"

"Not you. How are you ? Where's the girl ?"

"Gone up to your brother's."

" Humph ! to gad about and idle with Louie, I suppose. Here, I've brought you some fish. Caught it at daylight this morning. Ring for a dish."

"It's very kind and thoughtful of you, Luke Vine," said Mrs. Van Heldre, with her pink face dimpling as she rang the bell, and then trotted to the door, which she opened, and cried, "Bring in a large dish, Esther ! I always like to save the servants' legs if I can," she continued as she returned to her seat, while Van Heldre stood with his hands in his pockets, waiting. He knew his visitor.

Just then a neat-looking maid-servant entered with a large blue dish, and stood holding it by the door, gazing at the quaint-looking old man, sitting with the basket between his legs, and his heavy stick resting across his knees.

"Put it down and go."

The girl placed the dish on the table hurriedly, and left the room.

"See if she has gone."

"No fear," said Van Heldre, obeying, to humour his visitor. "I don't think my servants listen at doors."

"Don't trust 'em, or anybody else," said Uncle Luke with a grim look, as he opened his basket wide. "Going to trust her?"

"Well, I'm sure, Mr. Luke Vine!" cried Mrs. Van Heldre, "I believe you learn up rude things to say."

"He can't help it," said Van Heldre, laughing. "Yes," he continued, with a droll look at his wife, which took her frown away, "I think we'll trust her, Luke, my lad—as far as the fish is concerned."

"Eh! What?" said Uncle Luke, snatching his hands from his basket. "What do you mean?"

"That the dish is waiting for the bit of conger."

"Let it wait," said the old man snappishly. "You're too clever, Van—too clever. Look here; how are you getting on with that boy?"

"Oh, slowly. Rome was not built in a day."

"No," chuckled the old man, "no. Work away, and make him a useful member of society—like his aunt, eh, Mrs. Van."

"Useful!" cried Mrs. Van. "Ah."

Then old Luke chuckled, and drew the fish from the basket.

"Fine one, ain't it?" he said.

"A beauty," cried Mrs. Van Heldre ecstatically.

"Pshah!" ejaculated Uncle Luke. "Ma'am, you don't care for it a bit; but there's more than I want, and it will help keep your servants."

"It would, Luke," said Van Heldre, laughing, as the fish was laid in the dish, "but they will not touch it. Well?"

"Eh? What do you mean by well?" snorted the old man with a suspicious look.

"Out with it."

"Out with what?"

"What you have brought."

The two men gazed in each other's faces, the merchant looking half amused, the visitor annoyed; but his dry countenance softened

into a smile, and he turned to Mrs. Van
Heldre. "Artful!" he said dryly. "Don't
you find him too cunning to get on with?"

"I should think not indeed," said Mrs. Van
Heldre indignantly.

"Might have known you'd say that," sneered
Uncle Luke. "What a weak, foolish woman
you are!"

"Yes, I am, thank goodness! I wish you'd
have a little more of my foolishness in you,
Mr. Luke Vine. There, I beg your pardon.
What have you got there, shrimps?"

"Yes," said Uncle Luke grimly, as he
brought a brown paper parcel from the bottom
of his basket, where it had lain under the wet
piece of conger, whose stain was on the cover,
"some nice crisp fresh shrimps. Here, Van—
catch."

He threw the packet to his brother's old
friend and comrade, by whom it was deftly
caught, while Mrs. Van Heldre looked on in
a puzzled way.

"Put 'em in your safe till I find another
investment for 'em. Came down by post this
morning, and I don't like having 'em at home.
Out fishing so much."

"How much is there?" said Van Heldre,
opening the fishy brown paper, and taking

therefrom sundry crisp new Bank of England notes.

" Five hundred and fifty," said Uncle Luke. " Count 'em over."

This was already being done, Van Heldre having moistened a finger and begun handling the notes in regular bank-clerk style.

" All right ; five fifty," he said.

" And he said they were shrimps," said Mrs. Van Heldre.

" Eh ? I did ? " said Uncle Luke with a grim look and a twinkle of the eye. " Nonsense, it must have been you."

" Look here, Luke Vine," said Van Heldre ; " is it any use to try and teach you at your time of life ? "

" Not a bit : so don't try."

" But why expose yourself to all this trouble and risk ? Why didn't your broker send you a cheque ? "

" Because I wouldn't let him."

" Why not have a banking account, and do all your money transactions in an ordinary way ? "

" Because I like to do things in my own way. I don't trust bankers, nor anybody else."

" Except my husband," said Mrs. Van Heldre, beaming.

"Nonsense, ma'am, I don't trust him a bit. You do as I tell you, Van. Put those notes in your safe till I ask you for them. I had that bit of money in a company I doubted, so I sold out. I shall put it in something else soon."

"You're a queer fellow, Luke."

"Eh? I'm not the only one of my family, am I? What's to become of brother George when that young scapegrace has ruined him? What's to become of Louie, when we're all dead and buried, and out of all this worry and care? What's to become of my mad sister, who squandered her money on a French scamp, and made what she calls her heart bankrupt?"

"Nearly done questioning?" said Van Heldre, doubling the notes longwise.

"No, I haven't, and don't play with that money as if it was your wife's curl-papers."

Van Heldre shrugged his shoulders, and placed the notes in his pocket.

"And as I was saying when your husband interrupted me so rudely, Mrs. Van Heldre, what's to become of that boy by and by? Money's useful sometimes, though I don't want it myself."

"Ah! you needn't look at me, Mr. Luke

Vine. It's of no use for you to pretend to be a cynic with me."

"Never pretend anything, ma'am," said Uncle Luke, rising; "and don't be rude. I did mean to come in and have some conger-pie to-night; now I won't."

"No, you didn't mean to do anything of the sort, Luke Vine," said Mrs. Van Heldre tartly; "I know you better than that. If I've asked you to come and have a bit of dinner with us like a Christian once I've asked you five hundred times, and one might just as well ask the hard rock."

"Just as well, ma'am; just as well. There, I'm going. Take care of that money, Van. I shall think out a decent investment one of these days."

"When you want it there it is," said Van Heldre quietly.

"Hope it will be. And now look here: I want to know a little more about the Count."

"The Count?" said Mrs. Van Heldre.

"My nephew, ma'am. And I hope you feel highly honoured at having so distinguished a personage in your husband's service."

"What does he mean, dear?"

"Mean, ma'am? Why, you know how his

aunt has stuffed his head full of nonsense about French estates."

"Oh! that, and the old title," cried Mrs. Van Heldre. "There, don't say any more about it, for if there is anything that worries me, it's all that talk about French descents."

"Why, hang it, ma'am, you don't think your husband is a Frenchman, and that my sister, who has made it all the study of her life, is wrong?"

"I don't know and I don't care whether my husband's a Dutchman or a double Dutchman by birth; all I know is he's a very good husband to me and a good father to his child; and I thank God, Mr. Luke Vine, every night that things are just as they are; so that's all I've got to say."

"Tut—tut! tut—tut! This is all very dreadful, Van," said Uncle Luke, fastening his basket, and examining his old straw hat to see which was the best side to wear in front; "I can't stand any more of this. Here, do you want a bit of advice?"

"Yes, if it's good."

"Ah! I was forgetting about the Count. Keep the curb tight and keep him in use."

"I shall do both, Luke, for George's sake," said Van Heldre warmly.

"Good, lad!—I mean, more fool you!" said Uncle Luke, stumping out after ignoring extended hands and giving each a nod. "That's all."

He left the room, closing the door after him as loudly as he could without the shock being considered a bang; and directly after the front door was served in the same way, and they saw him pass the window.

"Odd fish, Luke," said Van Heldre.

"Odd! I sometimes think he's half mad."

"Nonsense, my dear; no more mad than Hamlet. Here he is again."

For the old man had come back, and was tapping the window-frame with his stick.

"What's the matter?" said Van Heldre, throwing open the window, when Uncle Luke thrust in the basket he carried and his stick, resting his arms on the window-sill.

"Don't keep that piece of conger in this hot room all the morning," he said, pointing with his stick.

"Why, goodness me, Luke Vine, how can you talk like that?" cried Mrs. Van Heldre indignantly.

"Easy enough, ma'am. Forgot my bit of advice," said Uncle Luke, speaking to his old friend, but talking at Mrs. Van Heldre.

" What is it ? "

"Send that girl of yours to a boarding-school."

" Bless my heart, Luke Vine, what for ? " cried the lady of the house. " Why, she finished two years ago."

" To keep her out of the way of George Vine's stupid boy, and because her mother's spoiling her. Morning."

# CHAPTER XIII.

## TO REAP THE WIND.

LATE dinner was nearly over—at least late according to the ideas of the West-country family, who sat down now directly Harry returned from his office work. Aunt Marguerite, after a week in her bedroom, had come down that day, the trouble with Liza exciting her; and that maiden had rather an unpleasant time as she waited at table, looking red-eyed and tearful, for Aunt Marguerite watched her with painful, basilisk-like glare all through the meal, the consequence being a series of mishaps and blunders, ending with the spilling of a glass dish of clotted cream.

With old-fashioned politeness, Aunt Marguerite tried to take Pradelle's attention from the accident.

"Are you going for a walk this evening, Mr. Pradelle?"

"Yes," he said; "I dare say we shall smoke a cigar together after the labours of the day."

Aunt Marguerite sighed and looked pained.

"Tobacco! Yes, Mr. Pradelle," she sighed; and she continued, in a low tone, "Do pray try to use your influence on poor Henri, to coax him from these bad pursuits."

Harry was talking cynically to his sister and Madelaine, who had been pressed by Vine to stay, a message having been sent down to the Van Heldres to that effect.

"The old story," he said to himself; and then, as he caught his sister's eye after she had gazed uneasily in the direction of her aunt; "yes, she's talking about me. Surely you don't mind that."

He, too, glanced now in Aunt Marguerite's direction, as Pradelle talked to her in a slow, impressive tone.

"Ah! no," said Aunt Marguerite, in a playful whisper, "nothing of the kind. A little boy and girl badinage in the past. Look for yourself, Mr. Pradelle; there is no warmth there! My nephew cannot marry a Dutch doll."

"Lovers' tiff, perhaps," said Pradelle.

"No, no," said Aunt Marguerite, shaking

her head confidently. "Harry is a little wild and changeable, but he pays great heed to my words and advice. Still I want your help, Mr. Pradelle. Human nature is weak. Harry must win back his French estates."

"Hear that, Louie?" said Harry, for Aunt Marguerite had slightly raised her voice.

"Yes, I heard," said Louise quietly.

"Aunt is sick of seeing her nephew engaged in a beggarly trade."

"For which Mr. Henry Vine seems much too good," said Madelaine to herself, as she darted an indignant glance at the young man. "Oh, Harry, what a weak, foolish boy you are! I don't love you a bit. It was all a mistake."

"I hate business," continued Harry, as he encountered her eyes fixed upon him.

"Yes," said Louise coldly, as an angry feeling of annoyance shot through her on her friend's behalf. "Harry has no higher ambition than to lead a lap-dog kind of life in attendance upon Aunt Marguerite, and listening to her stories of middle-aged chivalry."

"Thank goodness!" said Harry, as they rose from the table. "No, no, aunt, I don't want any coffee. I should stifle if I stopped here much longer."

Aunt Marguerite frowned as the young man declined the invitation to come to her side.

"Only be called a lap-dog again. Here, Vic, let's go and have a cigar down by the sea."

"Certainly," said Pradelle, smiling at all in turn.

"Yes, the room is warm," said the host, who had hardly spoken all through the dinner, being deep in thought upon one of his last discoveries.

Harry gave his sister a contemptuous look, which she returned with one half sorrowful, half pitying, from which he turned to glance at Madelaine, who was standing by her friend.

Aunt Marguerite smiled, for there was certainly the germ of an incurable rupture between these two, and she turned away her head to hide her triumph.

"She will never forgive him for speaking as he did about the beggarly trade." Then crossing with a graceful old-world carriage, she laid her hand on Madelaine's arm.

"Come into the drawing-room, my dear," she said, smiling, and to Madelaine it seemed that her bright, malicious-looking eyes were full of triumph. "You and I will have a good hard fight over genealogies, till you confess that I am right, and that your father and you have no claim to Huguenot descent."

"Oh no, Miss Vine," said the girl, laughing, "my father must fight his own battle. As for me, I give up. Perhaps you are right, and I am only a Dutch girl after all."

"Oh, I wish we were back in London!" cried Harry as they strolled along towards the cliff walk.

"Ah, this is a dead-and-alive place, and no mistake," said Pradelle.

"Why don't you leave it, then?" said Harry sulkily. "You are free."

"No, I am not. I don't like to see a friend going to the bad; and besides, I have your aunt's commission to try and save you from sinking down into a miserable tradesman."

"Why don't you save me, then?"

"That's just like you. Look here, sink all cowardice, and go up to the old boy like a Trojan. Plenty of money, hasn't he?"

"I suppose so. I don't know."

"He's sure to have."

"But he's such an old porcupine."

"Never mind. Suppose you do get a few pricks, what of that? Think of the future."

"But that venture must be all over now."

"What of that? You get the money and

I can find a dozen ways of investing it. Look here, Harry, you profess to be my friend, and to have confidence in my judgment, and yet you won't trust me."

" I trusted you over several things, and see how I lost."

" Come, that's unkind. A man can't always win. There, never look back, look forward. Show some fight, and make one good plunge to get out of that miserable shop-boy sort of life."

" Come along, then."

" You'll go up and ask him ? "

" Yes, if you'll back me up."

" Back you up, lad ? I should think I will. Lead on, I'll follow thee."

" We'll do it sensibly, then. If you speak before Uncle Luke in that theatrical way we shall come down faster than we go up."

" I'll talk to the old man like a young Solomon, and he shall say that never did youth choose more wisely for his friend than Harry Vine, otherwise Henri, Comte des Vignes."

" Look here," said Harry peevishly— " ' otherwise Comte des Vignes.' Why don't you say *alias* at once ? Why, if the old man heard that he'd want to know how long it was

since you were in a police court.    Here, you'd
better stay down here."

"All right, my dear fellow.    Anything to
help you on."

"No ; I'd rather you came too."

There was a pause in a niche of the rocks,
and then, after the scratching of a match, the
young men went up the cliff-path, smoking
furiously, as they prepared themselves for the
attack.

# CHAPTER XIV.

## DIOGENES IN HIS TUB.

UNCLE LUKE was in very good spirits. He had rid himself of his incubus, as he called the sum of money, and though he would not own it, he always felt better when he had had a little converse with his fellow-creatures. His lonely life was very miserable, and the more so that he insisted upon its being the highest form of happiness to exist in hermit fashion, as the old saints proved.

The desolate hut in its rocky niche looked miserable when he climbed up back on his return from Van Heldre's, so he stopped by the granite wall and smiled.

"Finest prospect in all Cornwall," he said, half aloud; "freshest air. Should like to blow up Leslie's works, though."

The door was locked, but it yielded to the heavy key which secured it against visitors, though they were very rare upon that rocky shelf.

He was the more surprised then, after his frugal mid-day meal, by a sharp rapping at the door, and on going he stared angrily at the two sturdy sailor-dressed pedlars, who were resting their packs on the low granite wall.

"Can we sell a bit o' 'bacco, or a pound o' tea, master?" said the man who had won over Liza to the purchase of his coloured silk.

"Bang!"

That was Uncle Luke's answer as the man spoke to him and his fellow swept the interior of the cottage with one quick glance.

"Steal as soon as sell any day," grumbled Uncle Luke. "Tobacco and tea, indeed!"

Outside one of the men gave his companion a wink and a laugh, as he shouldered his pack, while the other chuckled and followed his example.

Meanwhile Uncle Luke had seated himself at his rough deal table, and written a long business letter to his lawyer in London.

This missive he read over twice, made an addition to the paragraph dealing most particularly with the mortgage on which he had been invited to lend, and then carefully folded

the square post-paper he used in old-fashioned
letter shape, tucking one end into the other
from objects of economy, so as to dispense
with envelopes, but necessitating all the same
the use of sealing-wax and a light.

However, it pleased him to think that he
was saving, and he lit a very thin candle, took
the stick of red wax from a drawer, a curious
old-fashioned signet gold ring bearing the
family crest from a nail where it hung over
the fireplace, and then, sitting down as if to
some very important piece of business, he
burned his wax, laid on a liberal quantity, and
then impressed the seal. This done, the ring
was hung once more upon its nail, and the old
man stood gazing at it and thinking. The
next minute he took down the ring, and
slipped it on one of his fingers, and worked it
up and down, trying it on another finger, and
then going back to the first.

" Used to fit too tightly," he said ; "now
one's fingers are little more than bone."

He held up the ring to the light, his white
hand looking very thin and wasted, and the
worn gold glistened and the old engraved
blood-stone showed its design almost as clearly
as when it was first cut.

" ' Roy et Foy !' " muttered the old man,

reading the motto beneath the crest. "Bit of vanity. Margaret asked where it was, last time I saw her. Let's see; I lost you twice, once when I wore you as I was fishing off the pier, and once on the black rock you slipped off my bony finger, and each time the sea washed you into a crack."

He smiled as he gazed at the ring, and there was a pleasant, handsome trace of what he had been as a young man in his refined features.

"Please the young dog—old family ring," he muttered. "Might sell it and make a pound. No, he may have it when I'm gone. Can't be so very long."

He hung the ring upon the nail once more, and spent the rest of the afternoon gazing out to sea, sometimes running over the past, but more often looking out for the glistening and flashing of the sea beneath where a flock of gulls were hovering over some shoal of fish.

It was quite evening when there was a staid, heavy step and the click of nailed boots as the old fishwoman came toiling up the cliff-path, her basket on her back, and the band which supported it across her brow.

"Any fish to sell, Master Vine?" she said

in a sing-song tone. "I looked down the
pier, but you weren't there."

"How could I be there when I'm up here,
Poll Perrow?"

"Ah, to be sure; how could you?" said
the old woman, trying to nod her head, but
without performing the feat, on account of her
basket. "Got any fish to sell?"

"No. Yes," said the old man.

"That's right. I want some to-night. Will
you go and fetch it?"

"Yes. Stop there," said Uncle Luke sourly,
as he saw a chance of making a few pence, and
wondered whether he would get enough from
his customer.

"Mind my sitting down inside, Master
Luke Vine, sir? It's hot, and I'm tired; and
it's a long way up here."

"Why do you come, then?"

"Wanted to say a few words to you about
my gal when we've done our bit o' trade."

"Come in and sit down, then," said the
old man gruffly. And his visitor slipped the
leather band from her forehead, set her basket
on the granite wall, and went into the kitchen-
like room, wiping her brow as she seated
herself in the old rush-bottomed chair.

"I'll fetch it here," said Uncle Luke, and

he went round to the back, to return directly with the second half of the conger.

"There," said the old man eagerly, "how much for that?"

"Oh, I can't buy half a conger, Mr. Luke Vine, sir; and I don't know as I'd have took it if it had been whole."

"Then be off, and don't come bothering me," grunted the old man snappishly.

"Don't be cross, master; you've no call to be. You never have no gashly troubles to worry you."

"No, nor don't mean to have. What's the matter now?"

"My gal!"

"Serve you right. No business to have married. You never saw me make such a fool of myself."

"No, master, never; but when you've got gals you must do your best for 'em."

"Humph! what's the matter?"

Poll Perrow looked slowly round the ill-furnished, untidy place.

"You want a woman here, Master Luke Vine, sir," she said at last.

"Don't talk nonsense!"

"It aren't nonsense, Master Luke Vine, and you know it. You want your bed made proper, and your washing done, and your place scrubbed. Now why don't you let my gal come up every morning to do these things?"

"Look here," said Uncle Luke, "what is it you mean?"

"She's got into a scrape at Mr. Vine's, sir—something about some money being missing—and I suppose she'll have to come home, so I want to get her something to do."

"Oh, she isn't honest enough for my brother's house, but she's honest enough for mine."

"Oh, the gal's honest enough. It's all a mistake. But I can't afford to keep her at home, so, seeing as we'd had dealings together, I thought you'd oblige me and take her here."

"Seeing as we'd had dealings together!" grumbled Uncle Luke.

"Everything is so untidy-like, sir," said the old fish-dealer, looking round. "Down at your brother's there's everything a gentleman could wish for, but as to your place—why, there: it's worse than mine."

"Look here, Poll Perrow," said the old eccentricity fiercely, "this is my place, and I do in it just as I like. I don't want your girl to come and tidy my place, and I don't want you to come and bother me, so be off.

There's a letter; take it down and post it for me : and there's a penny for your trouble."

"Thank ye, master. Penny saved is a penny got; but Mr. George Vine would have given me sixpence—I'm not sure he wouldn't have given me a shilling. Miss Louise would."

Uncle Luke was already pointing at the door, towards which the woman moved unwillingly.

"Let me come up to-morrow and ask you, Mr. Luke, sir. Perhaps you'll be in a better temper then."

"Better temper!" he cried wrathfully. "I'm always in a better temper. Because I refuse to ruin myself by having your great, idle girl to eat me out of house and home, I'm not in a good temper, eh? There, be off! or I shall say something unpleasant."

"I'm a-going, sir. It's all because I wouldn't buy half a fish, as I should have had thrown on my hands, and been obliged to eat myself. Look here, sir," cried the woman, as she adjusted the strap of her basket, "if I buy the bit of fish will you take the poor gal then?"

"No!" cried Uncle Luke, slamming the door, as the woman stood with her basket once more upon her back.

"Humph!" exclaimed the old woman, as

she thrust the penny in her pocket, and then hesitated as to where she should place the letter.

While she was considering, the little window was opened and Uncle Luke's head appeared.

"Mind you don't lose that letter."

"Never you fear about that," said the old woman; and as if from a bright inspiration she pitched it over her head into her basket, and then trudged away.

"She'll lose that letter as sure as fate," grunted Uncle Luke. "Well, there's nothing in it to mind. Now I suppose I can have a little peace, and— Who's this?"

He leaned a little farther out of his window, so as to bring a curve of the cliff-path well into view.

"My beautiful nephew and that parasite. Going up to Leslie, I suppose—to smoke. Waste and debauchery—smoking."

He shut the window sharply, and settled himself down with his back to it, determined not to see his nephew pass; but five minutes later there was a sharp rapping at the door.

"Uncle Luke! Uncle!"

The old man made no reply.

"Here, Uncle Luke. I know you're at home; the old woman said so."

"Hang that old woman!" grumbled Uncle Luke; and in response to a fresh call he rose, and opened his door with a snatch.

"Now then, what is it? I'm just going to bed."

"Bed at this time of the day?" cried Harry cheerfully. "Why you couldn't go to sleep if you did go."

"Why not?" snapped the old man; "you can in the mornings—over the ledger."

Harry winced, but he turned off the malicious remark with a laugh.

"Uncle loves his joke, Pradelle," he said. "Come, uncle, I don't often visit you; ask us in."

"No, you don't often visit me, Harry," said the old man, looking at him searchingly; "and when you do come it's because you want something."

Harry winced again, for the old man's words cut deeply.

"Oh, nonsense, uncle! Pradelle and I were having a stroll, and we thought we'd drop in here and smoke a cigar with you."

"Very kind," said the old man, looking meaningly [from one to the other. "Missed meeting the girls, or have they snubbed you and sent you about your business?"

"Have a cigar, uncle?" said Harry, holding out his case. "I tell you we came on purpose to see you."

"Humph!" said Uncle Luke, taking the handsome morocco cigar-case, and turning it over and over with great interest. "How much did that cost?"

"Don't remember now; fifteen shillings I think."

"Ah," said Uncle Luke, pressing the snap and opening it. "One, two, three, four; how much do these cigars cost?"

"Only fourpence, uncle; can't afford better ones."

"And a cigar lasts—how long?"

"Oh, I make one last three-quarters of an hour, because I smoke very slowly. Try one."

"No, thankye; can't afford such luxuries, my boy," said the old man, shutting the case with a snap, and returning it. "That case and the cigars there cost nearly a pound. Your income must be rising fast."

Harry and Pradelle exchanged glances. The reception did not promise well for a loan.

"Cigar does you good sometimes."

"Harry," said the old man, laughing and pointing at the case.

"What's the matter, uncle?" said Harry eagerly; "want one?"

"No, no. Why didn't you have it put on there?"

"What?"

"Crest and motto, and your title—Comte des Vignes. You might lose it, and then people would know where to take it."

"Don't chaff a fellow, uncle," said Harry, colouring. "Here, we may come and sit down, mayn't we?"

"Oh, certainly, if your friend will condescend to take a seat in my homely place."

"Only too happy, Mr. Luke Vine."

"Are you now? Shouldn't have thought it," sneered the old man. "No wine to offer you, sir; no brandy and soda; that's the stuff young men drink now, isn't it?"

"Don't name it, my dear sir; don't name it," said Pradelle, with an attempt at heartiness that made the old man half close his eyes. "Harry and I only came up for a stroll. Besides, we've just dined."

"Have you? That's a good job, because I've only a bit of conger in the house, and that isn't cooked. Come in and sit down, sir. You, Harry, you'll have to sit down on that old oak chest."

"Anywhere will do for me, uncle. May we smoke?"

"Oh, yes, as fast as you like; it's too slow a poison for you to die up here."

"Hope so," said Harry, whose mission and the climb had made him very warm.

"Now, then," said Uncle Luke, fixing his eyes on Pradelle—like gimlets, as that gentleman observed on the way back; "what is it?"

"Eh? I beg pardon; the business here is Harry's."

"Be fair, Vic," said Harry, shortly; "the business appertains to both."

"Does it really," said Uncle Luke, with a mock display of interest.

"Yes, uncle," said the nephew, uneasily, as he sat twiddling the gold locket attached to his chain, and his voice sounded husky; "it relates to both."

"Really!" said Uncle Luke, with provoking solemnity, as he looked from one to the other. "Well, I was young myself once. Now, look here; can I make a shrewd guess at what you want?"

"I'll be bound to say you could, sir," said Pradelle, in despite of an angry look from Harry, who knew his uncle better, and foresaw a trap.

"Then I'll guess," said the old man, smiling pleasantly; "you want some money."

"Yes, uncle, you're right," said Harry, as cautiously as a fencer preparing for a thrust from an expert handler of the foils.

"Hah! I thought I was. Well, young men always were so. Want a little money to spend, eh?"

"Well, uncle, I——"

"Wait a minute, my boy," said the old man, seriously; "let me see. I don't want to disappoint you and your friend as you've come all this way. Your father wouldn't let you have any, I suppose?"

"Haven't asked him, sir."

"That's right, Harry," said the old man, earnestly; "don't, my boy, don't. George always was close with his money. Well, I'll see what I can do. How much do you want to spend—a shilling?"

"Hang it all, uncle!" cried Harry angrily, and nearly tearing off his locket, "don't talk to me as if I were a little boy. I want a hundred pounds."

"Yes, sir, a hundred pounds," said Pradelle.

"A hundred, eh? A hundred pounds. Do you, now?" said Uncle Luke, without seeming in the slightest degree surprised.

"The fact is, uncle, my friend Pradelle here is always hearing of openings for making a little money by speculations, and we have a chance now that would make large returns for our venture."

"Hum! hah!" ejaculated Uncle Luke, as he looked at Pradelle in a quiet, almost appealing way. "Let me see, Mr. Pradelle. You are a man of property, are you not!"

"Well, sir, hardly that," said Pradelle nonchalantly; and he rose, placed his elbows on the rough chimney-piece, and leaned back with his legs crossed as he looked down at Uncle Luke. "My little bit of an estate brings me in a very small income."

"Estate here?"

'No, no; in France, near Marseilles."

"That's awkward; a long way off."

"Go on," said Pradelle with his eyes, as he glanced at Harry.

"No good. Making fun of us," said Harry's return look; and the old man's eyes glistened.

"Hundred pounds. Speculation, of course?"

"Hardly fair to call it speculation, it is so safe," said Pradelle, in face of a frown from his friend.

"Hum! A hundred pounds—a hundred

pounds," said Uncle Luke thoughtfully. " It's
a good deal of money."

" Oh, dear me, no, sir," said Pradelle.  " In
business matters a mere trifle."

" Ah ! you see I'm not a business man.
Why don't you lend it to my nephew, Mr.
Pradelle ?"

" I—I'm—well—er—really, I—  The fact
is, sir, every shilling I have is locked up."

" Then I should advise you to lose the key,
Mr. Pradelle," chuckled the old man, " or you
may be tempted to spend it."

" You're playing with us, uncle," cried
Harry.  " Look here, will you lend me a
hundred ?  I promise you faithfully I'll pay
it to you back."

" Oh ! of course, of course, my dear
boy."

" Then you'll lend it to me ?"

" Lend you a hundred ?  My dear boy, I
haven't a hundred pounds to lend you.  And
see how happy I am without !"

" Well, then, fifty, uncle.  I'll make that
do."

" Come, I like that, Harry," cried the old
man, fixing Pradelle with his eye.  " There's
something frank and generous about it.  It's
brave, too ; isn't it, sir ?"

"Yes, sir. Harry's as frank and good-hearted a lad as ever stepped."

"Thank you, Mr. Pradelle. It's very good of you to say so."

"Come along, Vic," said Harry.

"Don't hurry, my dear boy. So you have an estate in France, have you, Mr. Pradelle?"

"Yes, sir."

"Humph; so has Harry—at least he will have some day, I suppose. Yes, he is going to get it out of the usurper's hands—usurper is the word, isn't it, Harry?"

Harry gave a kick out with one leg.

"Yes, usurper is the word. He's going to get the estate some day, Mr. Pradelle; and then he is going to be a Count. Of course he will have to give up being Mr. Van Heldre's clerk then."

"Look here, uncle," cried the young man hotly; "if you will not lend me the money, you needn't insult me before my friend."

"Insult you, my dear boy? Not I. What a peppery fellow you are! Now your aunt will tell you that this is your fine old French aristocratic blood effervescing; but it can't be good for you."

"Come along, Vic," said Harry.

"Oh, of course," said Pradelle. "I'm sorry,

though.  Fifty pounds isn't much, sir ; perhaps you'll think it over."

" Eh ? think it over.  Of course I shall.
Sorry I can't oblige you, gentlemen.  Good
evening."

" Grinning at us all the time—a miserable
old miser !" said Harry, as they began to
walk back.  " He'd have done it if you hadn't
made such a mess of it, Vic, with your free-
and-easy way."

" It's precious vexatious, Harry ; but take
care, or you'll sling that locket out to sea,"
said Pradelle, after they had been walking
for about ten minutes.  " You'll have to think
about my proposal.  You can't go on like
this."

" No," said Harry fiercely ; " I can't go on
like this, and I'll have the money somehow."

" Bravo !  That's spoken like a man who
means business.  Harry, if you keep to that
tone, we shall make a huge fortune apiece.
How will you get the money ?"

" I'll ask Duncan Leslie for it.  He can't
refuse me.  I should like to see him say ' No.'
He must and he shall."

" Then have a hundred, dear lad.  Don't
be content with fifty."

" I will not, you may depend upon that,"
cried Harry, " and——"

He stopped short, and turned white, then
red, and took half-a-dozen strides forward
towards where Madelaine Van Heldre was
seated upon one of the stone resting-places in
a niche in the cliff—the very one where
Duncan Leslie had had his unpleasant conversation with Aunt Marguerite.

The presence of his sister's companion, in
spite of their being slightly at odds, might
have been considered pleasant to Harry Vine ;
and at any other time it would have been, but
in this instance she was bending slightly
forward, and listening to Duncan Leslie, who
was standing with his back to the young
men.

Only a minute before, and Harry Vine had
determined that with the power given by
Leslie's evident attachment to his sister, he
would make that gentleman open his cash-box
or write a cheque on the Penzance bank for a
hundred pounds.

The scene before him altered Harry Vine's
ideas, and sent the blood surging up to his
brain.

He stepped right up to Madelaine, giving
Leslie a furious glance as that gentleman

turned, and without the slightest preface, exclaimed—

"Look here, Madelaine, it's time you were at home. Come along with me."

Madelaine flushed as she rose; and her lips parted as if to speak, but Leslie interposed.

"Excuse me, Miss Van Heldre, I do not think you need reply to such a remark as that."

"Who are you?" roared Harry, bursting into a fit of passion that was schoolboy-like in its heat and folly. "Say another word, sir, and I'll pitch you off the cliff into the sea."

"Here, steady, old fellow, steady!" whispered Pradelle; and he laid his hand on his companion's arm.

"You mind your own business, Vic; and as for you——"

He stopped, for he could say no more. Leslie had quite ignored his presence, turning his back and offering his arm to Madelaine.

"Shall I walk home with you, Miss Van Heldre?" he said.

For answer, and without so much as looking at Harry Vine, Madelaine took the offered arm, and Pradelle tightened his hold as the couple walked away.

The grasp was needless, for Harry's rage

was evaporating fast, and giving place to a
desolate sensation of despair.

"Look here," said Pradelle; "you've kicked
that over. You can't ask him now."

"No," said Harry, gazing at the departing
figures, and trying to call up something about
the fair daughters of France; "no, I can't ask
him now."

"Then look here, old fellow, I can't stand
by and see you thrown over by everybody
like this. You know what your prospects are
on your own relative's showing, not mine;
and you know what can be done if we have
the money. You are not fit for this place,
and I say you shall get out of it. Now then,
you know how it can be done. Just a loan
for a few weeks. Will you, or will you not?"

Harry turned upon him a face that was
ghastly pale. "But if," he whispered hoarsely,
"if we should fail?"

"Fail? You shan't fail."

"One hundred," said Harry, hoarsely.

"Well, I suppose so. We'll make that do.
Now then, I'm not going to waste time. Is it
yes or no?"

Harry Vine felt a peculiar humming in the
head, his mouth was hot and dry, and his lips
felt parched. He looked Pradelle in the face,

as if pleading to be let off, but there was only a cunning, insistent smile to meet him there, and once more the question came in a sharp whisper,

"Yes or no?"

"Yes," said Harry; and as soon as he had said that word, it was as if a black cloud had gathered about his life.

# CHAPTER XV.

DUNCAN LESLIE was a sturdy, manly young fellow in his way, but he had arrived at a weak period. He thought over his position, and what life would become had he a wife at home he really loved ; and in spite of various displays of reserve, and the sneers, hints, and lastly the plain declaration that Louise was to marry some French gentleman of good family and position, Duncan found himself declaring that his ideas were folly one hour, and the next he was vowing that he would not give up, but that he would win in spite of all the Frenchmen on the face of the earth.

" I must have a walk," he used to say. " If I stop poring over books now, I shall be quite thick-headed to-morrow. A man must study his health."

So Duncan Leslie studied his health, and started off that evening in a different direction to the Vines'; and then, in spite of himself, began to make a curve, one which grew smaller and smaller as he walked thoughtfully on.

"I don't see why I should not call," he said to himself. "There's no harm in that. Wish I had found some curious sea-anemone; I could go and ask the old man what it was—and have her sweet clear eyes reading me through and through. I should feel that I had lowered myself in her sight."

"No," he said, emphatically; "I'll be straightforward and manly over it if I can."

"Hang that old woman! She doesn't like me. There's a peculiarly malicious look in her eyes whenever we meet. Sneering fashion, something like her old brother, only he seems honest and she does not. I'd give something to know whether Louise cares for that French fellow. If she doesn't, why should she be condemned to a life of misery? Could I make her any happier?"

"I'll go home now."

"No, I—I will not; I'll call."

These questions had been scattered over Duncan Leslie's walk, and the making up of his mind displayed in the last words was three-quarters of an hour after the first.

"I'm no better than a weak boy," he said,

as he strode along manfully now. "I make mountains of molehills. What can be more natural and neighbourly than for me to drop in, as I am going to do, for a chat with old Vine?"

There was still that peculiar feeling of consciousness, though, to trouble him, as he knocked, and was admitted by Liza, whose eyelids were nearly as red as the ribbon she had bought.

The next minute he was in the pleasant homely drawing-room, feeling a glow of love and pride, and ready to do battle with any De Ligny in France for the possession of the prize whose soft warm hand rested for a few moments in his.

"Ah, Miss Van Heldre," he said, as he shook hands with her in turn, and his face lit up and a feeling of satisfaction thrilled him, for there was something in matter-of-fact Madelaine that gave him confidence.

Aunt Marguerite's eyes twinkled with satisfaction, as she saw the cordial greeting, and built up a future of her own materials.

"Miss Marguerite," said the young man ceremoniously, as he touched the extended hand, manipulated so that he should only grasp the tips; and, as he saluted, Leslie could not help thinking philosophically upon the different sensations following the touch of a hand.

A growing chill was coming over the visit, and Leslie was beginning to feel as awkward as a sturdy well-grown young tree might, if suddenly transplanted from a warm corner to a situation facing an iceberg, when the old naturalist handed a chair for his visitor.

"Glad to see you, Leslie," he said; "sit down."

"You will take some tea, Mr. Leslie?"

Hah! The moment before the young man had felt ready to beat an ignominious retreat, but as soon as the voice of Louise Vine rang in his ears with that simple homely question, he looked up manfully, declared that he would take some tea, and in spite of himself glanced at Aunt Marguerite's tightening lips, his eyes seeming to say, "Now, then, march out a brigade of De Lignys if you like."

"And sugar, Mr. Leslie?"

"And sugar," he said, for he was ready to accept any sweets she would give.

Then he took the cup of tea, looked in the eyes that met his very frankly and pleasantly, and then his own rested upon a quaint-looking cornelian locket, which was evidently French.

There was nothing to an ordinary looker-on in that piece of jewellery, but somehow it troubled Duncan Leslie : and as he turned to speak to Aunt Marguerite, he felt that she had read his thoughts, and her lips had relaxed into a smile.

"Well, George, if you do not mind Mr. Leslie hearing, I do not," said Aunt Marguerite. "I must reiterate that the poor boy is growing every day more despondent and unhappy."

"Nonsense, Margaret!"

"Ah, you may say nonsense, my good brother, but I understand his nature better than you. Yes, my dear," she continued, "such a trade as that carried on by Mr. Van Heldre is not a suitable avocation for your son."

"Hah!" sighed Vine.

"Now, you are a tradesman, Mr. Leslie—" continued Aunt Marguerite.

"Eh? I, a tradesman?" said Leslie, looking at her wonderingly. "Yes, of course : I suppose so ; I trade in copper and tin."

"Yes, a tradesman, Mr. Leslie ; but you have your perceptions, you have seen, and you know my nephew. Now, answer me honestly, is Mr. Van Heldre's business suit-

able to a young man with such an ancestry as
Henri's ? "

Louise watched him wonderingly, and her
lips parted as she hung upon his words.

" Well, really, madam," he began.

" Ah," she said, " you shrink. His French
ancestors would have scorned such a pursuit."

" Oh, no," said Leslie, " I do not shrink;
and as to that, I think it would have been
very stupid of his French ancestors. Trading
in tin is a very ancient and honourable business. Let me see, it was the Phœnicians,
was it not, who used to come to our ports
for the metal in question? They were not
above trading in tin and Tyrian dye."

Aunt Marguerite turned up her eyes.

" And a metal is a metal. For my part, it
seems quite as good a pursuit to trade in tin
as in silver or gold."

Aunt Marguerite gave the young man a
pitying, contemptuous look, which made
Louise bite her lip.

" Aunt, dear," she said hurriedly, "let me
give you some more tea."

" I was not discussing tea, my dear, but
your brother's future; and pray, my dear
child," she continued, turning suddenly upon
Madelaine with an irritating smile, " pray do

not think I am disparaging your worthy father and his business affairs."

" Oh, no, Miss Vine."

" Miss *Marguerite* Vine, my child, if you will be so good. Oh, by the way, has your father heard any news of his ship ? "

" Not yet, Miss Marguerite," said Madelaine quietly.

" Dear me, I am very sorry. It would be so serious a loss for him, Mr. Leslie, if the ship did not come safe to port."

" Yes, of course," said Leslie ; " but I should suppose, Miss Van Heldre, that your father is well insured."

" Yes," said Madelaine quietly.

" There, never mind about Van Heldre's ship," said Vine pleasantly. " Don't croak like a Cassandra, Margaret ; and as to Harry, a year or two in a good solid business will not do him any harm, eh, Leslie ? "

" I should say it would do him a world of good."

" My nephew is not to be judged in the same light as a young man who is to be brought up as a tradesman," said Aunt Marguerite, with dignity.

" Only a tradesman's son, my dear."

" The descendant of a long line of ennobled

gentry, George ; a fact you always will forget,"
said Aunt Marguerite, rising and leaving the
room, giving Leslie, who opened the door, a
*Minuet de la Cour* courtesy on the threshold,
and then rustling across the hall.

Her brother took it all as a matter of course.
Once that Marguerite had ceased speaking the
matter dropped, to make way for something
far more important in the naturalist's eyes—
the contents of one of his glass aquaria ; but
Louise, to remove the cloud her aunt had left
behind, hastily kept the ball rolling.

" Don't think any more about aunt's remarks, Madelaine. Harry is a good fellow,
but he would be discontented anywhere
sometimes."

" I do not think he would be discontented
now," she replied, "if his aunt would leave
him alone."

" It is very foolish of him to think of what
she says."

" Of course it is irksome to him at first,"
continued Madelaine ; " but my father is not
exacting. It is the hours at the desk that
trouble your brother most."

" I wish I could see him contented," sighed
Louise. " I'd give anything to see him settle
down."

A very simple wish, which went right to Duncan Leslie's heart, and set him thinking so deeply that for the rest of his visit he was silent, and almost constrained—a state which Madelaine noted as she rose.

"Must you go so soon, dear?" said Louise consciously, for a terrible thought crossed her mind, and sent the blood surging to her cheeks —Madelaine was scheming to leave her and the visitor alone.

"Yes; they will be expecting me back," said Madelaine, smiling as she grasped her friend's thoughts; and then to herself, "Oh, you stupid fellow!"

For Leslie rose at once.

"And I must be going too. Let's see, I am walking your way, Miss Van Heldre. May I see you home?"

"I——"

"Yes, do, Mr. Leslie," said Louise quietly.

"Ah! I will," he said hastily. "I want a chat with your father, too."

Madelaine would have avoided the escort, but she could only have done this at the expense of making a fuss; so merely said "Very well;" and went off with Louise to put on her hat and mantle, leaving Leslie alone with his host, who was seated by the window with a watchmaker's glass in his eye, making use of the remaining light for the study of some wonderful marine form.

"She would give anything to see her brother settled down," said Leslie to himself, over and over again. "Well, why not?"

Five minutes later he and Madelaine were going along the main street, with Louise watching them from behind her father's chair, and wondering why she did not feel so happy as she did half an hour before; and Aunt Marguerite gazing from her open window.

"Ah!" said the old lady; "that's better. Birds of a feather do flock together, after all."

But the flocking pair had no such thoughts as those with which they were given credit, for directly they were outside, Duncan Leslie set Madelaine's heart beating by his first words.

"Look here," he said, "I want to take you into my counsel, Miss Van Heldre, because you have so much sound common sense."

"Is that meant for a compliment, Mr. Leslie?"

"No; I never pay compliments. Look

here," he said bluntly, "you take an interest in Harry Vine."

Madelaine was silent.

"That means yes," said Leslie. "Now to be perfectly plain with you, Miss Van Heldre, so do I; and I want to serve him if I can."

"Yes?" said Madelaine, growing more deeply interested.

"Yes, it is—as the sailors say. Now it's very plain that he is not contented where he is."

"I'm afraid not."

"What do you say to this?—I will not be a sham—I want to serve him for reasons which I dare say you guess; reasons of which I am not in the least ashamed. Now what do you think of this? How would he be with me?"

Madelaine flushed with pleasure.

"I cannot say. Is this a sudden resolve?"

"Quite. I never thought of such a thing till I went there."

"Then take time to think it over, Mr. Leslie."

"Good advice; but it is a thing that requires very little thought. I cannot say what arrangements I should make—that would require consideration—but I should not tie him to a desk. He would have the overlooking of a lot of men, and I should try to make him as happy as I could."

"Oh, Mr. Leslie!" said Madelaine, rather excitedly.

"Pray do not think I am slighting your father, or looking down upon what he has done, which, speaking as a blunt man, is very self-sacrificing."

"As it would be on your part."

"On mine? Oh, no," said Leslie frankly. "When a man has such an *arrière pensée* as I have, there is no self-sacrifice. There, you see I am perfectly plain."

"And I esteem you all the more for it."

The conversation extended, and in quite a long discussion everything was forgotten but the subject in hand, till Leslie said :—

"There, you had better sit down and rest for a few minutes. You are quite out of breath."

Madelaine looked startled, for she had been so intent upon their conversation that she had not heeded their going up the cliff walk.

"Sit down," said Leslie; and she obeyed. "Get your breath, and we'll walk back to your house together ; but what do you think of it all ? "

" I cannot help thinking that it would for many reasons be better."

" So do I," said Leslie, " in spite of the risk."

" Risk ? "

" Yes. Suppose I get into an imbroglio with Master Harry? He's as peppery as can be. How then ? "

" You will be firm and forbearing," said Madelaine gravely. " I have no fear."

" Well, I have. I know myself better than you know me," said Leslie, placing a foot on the seat and resting his arm on his knee, as he spoke thoughtfully. " I am a very hot-headed kind of Highlander by descent, and there's no knowing what might happen. Now one more question. Shall I open fire on your father to-night ? "

" That requires more consideration," said Madelaine. " We will talk that over as we go back. Here is Harry," she said quickly, as that gentleman suddenly burst upon them ; and the walk back to Van Heldre's was accomplished without the discussion.

" I'm afraid I've made a very great mistake, Miss Van Heldre," said Leslie, as they neared the house.

"Don't say that," she replied.    "It was most unfortunate."

"But you will soon set that right?" he added, after a pause.

"I don't know," said Madelaine quietly. "You will come in?"

"No; not this evening. We had better both have a grand think before anything is said."

"Yes," said Madelaine ; and they parted at the door—to think.

"Why, John," said Mrs. Van Heldre, turning from the window to gaze in her husband's face, "did you see that?"

"Yes," said Van Heldre shortly; "quite plainly."

"But what does it mean?"

"Human nature."

"But I thought, dear——"

"So did I, and now I think quite differently."

"Well, really, I must speak to Madelaine : it is so——"

"Silence!" said Van Heldre sternly. "Madelaine is not a child now. Wait, wife, and she will speak to us."

# CHAPTER XVI.

## IN A WEST COAST GALE.

"That project is knocked over as if it were a card house," said Duncan Leslie, as he reached home, and sat thinking of Louise and her brother.

He looked out to see that in a very short time the total aspect of the sea had changed. The sky had become overcast, and in the dim light the white horses of the Atlantic were displaying their manes.

"Very awkward run for the harbour to-night," he said, as he returned to his seat. "Can't be pleasant to be a ship-owner. I wonder whether Miss Marguerite Vine would consider that a more honourable way of making money?"

"Yes, a tradesman, I suppose. Well, why not? Better than being a descendant of some feudal gentleman whose sole idea of right was might."

" My word ! " he exclaimed ; " what a sudden gale to have sprung up. Heavy consumption of coal in the furnaces to-night. How this wind will make them roar."

He faced round to the window and sat listening as the wind shrieked, and howled, and beat at the panes, every now and then sending the raindrops pattering almost as loudly as hail. " Hope it will not blow down my chimney on the top yonder. Hah ! I ought to be glad that I have no ship to trouble me on a night like this."

" No," he said firmly, just as the wind had hurled itself with redoubled fury against the house ; " no, she does not give me a second thought. But I take heart of grace, for I can feel that she has never had that gentle little heart troubled by such thoughts. The Frenchman has not won her, and he never shall if I can help it. It's a fair race for both of us, and only one can win."

" My word ! What a night ! "

He walked to the window and looked out at the sombre sky, and listened to the roar of the rumbling billows before closing his casement and ringing.

" Is all fastened ? " he said to the servant. " You need not sit up.—I don't believe a dog would be out to-night, let alone a human being."

He was wrong; for just as he spoke a dark figure encased in oil-skins was sturdily making its way down the cliff-path to the town. It was hard work, and in places on the exposed cliff-side even dangerous, for the wind seemed to pounce upon the figure and try to tear it off; but after a few moments' pause the walk was continued, the town reached, and the wind-swept streets traversed without a soul being passed.

The figure passed on by the wharves and warehouses, and sheltered now from the wind made good way till, some distance ahead, a door was opened, a broad patch of light shone out on the wet cobble stones, Crampton's voice said, "Good-night," and the figure drew back into a deep doorway, and waited.

The old clerk had been to the principal inn, where, once a week, he visited his club, and drank one glass of Hollands and water, and smoked one pipe, talking mostly to one friend, to whom if urged he would relate one old story.

This was his one dissipation; and afterwards he performed one regular duty which took him close up to the watching figure which remained there almost breathless till Crampton had performed his regular duty and gone home.

It was ten minutes or a quarter of an hour before he passed that watching figure, which seemed to have sunk away in the darkness that grew more dense as the gale increased.

Morning at last, a slowly breaking dawn, and with it the various sea-going men slowly leaving their homes, to direct their steps in a long procession towards one point where the high cliff face formed a shelter from the south-west wind, and the great billows which rolled heavily in beneath the leaden sky. These came on with the regularity of machinery, to charge the cliffs at which they leaped with a hiss and a roar, and a boom like thunder, followed by a peculiar rattling, grumbling sound, as if the peal of thunder had been broken up into heavy pieces which were rolling over each other back toward the sea.

They were not pieces of thunder but huge boulders, which had been rolled over and over for generations to batter the cliffs, and then fall back down an inclined plane.

Quite a crowd had gathered on the broad, glistening patch of rugged granite, as soon as the day broke, and this crowd was ever augmenting, till quite a phalanx of oil-skin coats and tarpaulin hats presented its face to the thundering sea, while men shouted to each other, and swept the lead-coloured horizon with heavy glasses, or the naked hand-shaded eye, in search of some vessel trying to make the harbour, or in distress.

"She bites, this morning," said one old fisherman, shaking the spray from his dripping face after looking round the corner of a mass of sheltering rock.

"Ay, mate, and it aren't in me to tell you how glad I am my boat's up the harbour with her nose fast to a buoy," said another.

"There'll be widders and orphans in some ports 'fore nightfall."

"And thank the Lord that won't be in Hakemouth."

"I dunno so much about that," growled a heavy-looking man,' with a fringe of white hair round his face. "Every boat that sails out of this harbour arn't in port."

"That it is. Why, what's yer thinking about?"

"'Bout Van Heldre's brig, my lad."

"Ah," chorused half-a-dozen voices, "we didn't think o' she."

" Been doo days and days," said the white-fringed old fisherman ; " and if she's out yonder, I say, Lord ha' mercy on 'em all, Amen."

" Not had such a storm this time o' year since the Cape mail were wrecked off the Long Chain."

" Ah, and that warn't so bad as this. Bound to say the brig has put into Mount's Bay."

" And not a nice place either with the wind this how. Well, my lads, I say there's blessings and blessings, and we ought all to be werry thankful as we arn't ship-owners with wessels out yonder."

This was from the first man who had spoken ; but his words were not received with much favour, and as in a lull of the wind one of the men had to use a glass, he growled out,

" Well, I dunno 'bout sending one's ship to sea in such a storm, but I don't see as it's such a very great blessing not to have one of your own, speshly if she happened to be a brig like Mast' Van Heldre's ! "

" Hold your row," said a man beside him, as he drove his elbow into his ribs, and gave a side jerk of his head.

The man thus adjured turned sharply, and

saw close to him a sturdy-looking figure clothed from head to foot in black mackintosh, which glistened as it dripped with the showery spray.

"Ugly day, my lads."

"Ay, ay, sir ; much snugger in port than out yonder."

*Boom!* came a heavy blow from a wave, and the offing seemed to be obscured now by the drifting spray.

Van Heldre focussed a heavy binocular, and gazed out to sea long and carefully.

"Any one been up to the look-out ?" he said, as he lowered his glass.

"Two on us tried it, sir," said one of the men, "but the wind's offle up yonder, and you can't see nothing."

"Going to try it, sir ?" said another of the group.

Van Heldre nodded ; and he was on his way to a roughly-formed flight of granite steps which led up to the ruins of the old castle which had once defended the mouth of the harbour, when another mackintosh-clothed figure came up.

"Ah, Mr. Leslie," said Van Heldre, looking at the new-comer searchingly.

"Good morning," was the reply, "or I

should say bad morning. There'll be some mischief after this."

Van Heldre nodded, for conversation was painful, and passed on.

"Going up yonder?" shouted Leslie.

There was another nod, and under the circumstances, not pausing to ask permission, Leslie followed the old merchant, climbing the rough stone steps, and holding on tightly by the rail.

"Best look out, master," shouted one of the group. "Soon as you get atop roosh acrost and kneel down behind the old parry-putt."

It was a difficult climb and full of risk, for as they went higher they were more exposed, till as they reached the rough top which formed a platform, the wind seemed to rush at them as interlopers which it strove to sweep off and out to sea.

Van Heldre stood, glass in hand, holding on by a block of granite, his mackintosh tightly pressed to his figure in front, and filling out behind till it had a balloon-like aspect that seemed grotesque.

"I dare say I look as bad," Leslie muttered, as, taking the rough fisherman's advice, he bent down and crept under the shelter of the ancient parapet, a dwarf breastwork, with traces of the old crude bastions just visible, and here, to some extent, he was screened from the violence of the wind, and signed to Van Heldre to join him.

Leslie placed his hands to his mouth, and shouted through them,

" Hadn't you better come here, sir ? "

For the position seemed terribly insecure. They were on the summit of the rocky headland, with the sides going on three sides sheer down to the shore, on two of which sides the sea kept hurling huge waves of water, which seemed to make the rock quiver to its foundations. One side of the platform was protected by the old breastwork ; on the opposite the stones had crumbled away or fallen, and here there was a swift slope of about thirty feet to the cliff edge.

It was at the top of this slope that Van Heldre stood gazing out to sea.

Leslie, as he watched him, felt a curious premonition of danger, and gathered himself together involuntarily, ready for a spring.

The danger he anticipated was not long in making its demand upon him, for all at once there was a tremendous gust, as if an atmospheric wave had risen up to spring at the man standing on high as if daring the fury of the tempest; and in spite of Van Heldre's sturdy frame he completely lost his balance. He staggered for a moment, and, but for his presence of mind in throwing himself down, he would have been swept headlong down the swift slope to destruction.

As it was he managed to cling to the rocks, as the wind swept furiously over, and checked his downward progress for the moment. This would have been of little avail, for, buffeted by the wind, he was gliding slowly down, and but for Leslie's quickly rendered aid, it would only have been a matter of moments before he had been hurled down upon the rocks below.

Even as he staggered, Leslie mastered the peculiar feeling of inertia which attacked him, and, creeping rapidly over the intervening space, made a dash at the fluttering overcoat, caught it, twisted it rapidly, and held on.

Then for a space neither moved, for it was as if the storm was raging with redoubled fury at the chance of its victim being snatched away.

The lull seemed as if it would never come; and when it did Leslie felt afraid to stir lest the fragile material by which he supported

his companion should give way. In a few
moments, however, he was himself, and shout-
ing so as to make his voice plainly heard—for,
close as he was, his words seemed to be swept
away as uttered—he uttered a few short clear
orders, which were not obeyed.

"Do you hear?" he cried again, "Mr. Van
Heldre—quick!"

Still there was no reply by voice or action,
and it seemed as if the weight upon Leslie's
wrists was growing heavier moment by moment.
He yelled to him now, to act; and what
seemed to be a terrible time elapsed before
Van Heldre said hoarsely—

"One moment: better now. I felt paralyzed."

There was another terrible pause, during
which the storm beat upon them, the waves
thundered at the base of the rock, and even
at that height there came a rain of spray
which had run up the face of the rock and
swept over to where they lay.

"Now, quick!" said Van Heldre, as he lay
face downward, spread-eagled, as a sailor would
term it, against the face of the sloping granite.

What followed seemed to be a struggling
scramble, a tremendous effort, and then with
the wind shrieking round them, Van Heldre

reached the level, and crept slowly to the shelter of the parapet.

"Great heavens!" panted Leslie, as he lay there exhausted, and gazed wildly at his companion. "What an escape!"

There was no reply. Leslie thought that Van Heldre had fainted, for his eyes were nearly closed, and his face seemed to be drawn. Then he realized that his lips were moving slowly, as if in prayer.

"Hah!" the rescued man said at last, his words faintly heard in the tempest's din. "Thank God! For their sake—for their sake."

Then, holding out his hand, he pressed Leslie's in a firm strong grip.

"Leslie," he said, with his lips close to his companion's ear, "you have saved my life."

Neither spoke much after that, but they crouched there—in turn using the glass.

Once Van Heldre grasped his companion's arm, and pointed out to sea.

"A ship?" cried Leslie.

"No. Come down now."

Waiting till the wind had dropped for the moment, they reached the rough flight of steps, and on returning to the level found that the crowd had greatly increased; and among them Leslie saw Harry Vine and his companion.

"Can't see un, sir, can you?" shouted one of the men.

Van Heldre shook his head.

"I thought you wouldn't, sir," shouted another. "Capt'n Muskerry's too good a sailor to try and make this port in such a storm."

"Ay," shouted another. "She's safe behind the harbour wall at Penzaunce."

"I pray she may be," said Van Heldre. "Come up to my place and have some breakfast, Leslie, but not a word, mind, about the slip. I'll tell that my way."

"Then I decline to come," said Leslie, and after a hearty grip of the hand they parted.

"I thought he meant Vine's girl," said Van Heldre, as he walked along the wharves street, "but there is no accounting for these things."

"I ought to explain to him how it was I came to be walking with Miss Van Heldre," said Leslie to himself. "Good morning."

He had suddenly found himself face to face with Harry, who walked by, arm in arm with Pradelle, frowning and without a word, when just as they passed a corner the wind came with a tremendous burst, and but for Leslie's hand Harry Vine must have gone over into the harbour.

It was but the business of a moment, and Harry seemed to shake off the hand which held him with a tremendous grip and passed on.

"Might have said thank you," said Leslie, smiling. "I seem to be doing quite a business in saving people this morning, only they are of the wrong sex—there is no heroism. Hallo, Mr. Luke Vine. Come down to look at the storm?"

"Couldn't I have seen it better up at home?" shouted the old man. "Ugh! what a wind. Thought I was going to be blown off the cliff. I see your chimney still stands, worse luck. Going home?"

"No, no. One feels so much unsettled at such a time."

"Don't go home then. Stop with me."

Leslie looked at the quaint old man in rather an amused way, and then stopped with him to watch the tumbling billows off the point where his companion so often fished.

# CHAPTER XVII.

## THE NEWS.

THE day wore on with the storm now lulling slightly, now increasing in violence till it seemed as if the great rolling banks of green water must end by conquering in their attack, and sweeping away first the rough pier, and then the little twin towns on either side of the estuary. Nothing was visible seawards, but in a maritime place the attention of all is centred upon the expected, and in the full belief that sooner or later there would be a wreck, all masculine Hakemouth gathered in sheltered places to be on the watch.

Van Heldre and Leslie came into contact again that afternoon, and after a long look seaward, the merchant took the young man's arm.

"Come on to my place," he said quietly. "You'll come too, Luke Vine?"

"1? No, no," said the old fellow, shaking his head. "I want to stop and watch the sea go down."

His refusal was loud and demonstrative, but somehow there was a suggestion in it of a request to be asked again.

"Nonsense!" said Van Heldre. "You may as well come and take shelter for a while. You will not refuse, Leslie?"

"Thanks all the same, but I hope you will excuse me too," replied Leslie with his lips, but with an intense desire to go, for there was a possibility of Louise being at the house with Madelaine.

"I shall feel vexed if you refuse," said Van Heldre quietly. "Come along, Luke, and dine with us. I'm depressed and worried to-day; be a bit neighbourly if you can."

"Oh, I'll come," said the old man; "but it serves you right. Why can't you be content as I am, instead of venturing hundreds and hundreds of pounds in ships on the sea? Here, come along, Leslie, and let's eat and drink all we can to help him, the extravagant spendthrift."

Van Heldre smiled, and they went along to the house together.

"The boy in yonder at work?" said Uncle

Luke, giving a wag of his head toward the office.

"Yes," said Van Heldre, and ushered his visitors in, the closed door seeming directly after to shut out the din and confusion of the wind-swept street.

"There, throw your mackintoshes on that chair," said Van Heldre; and hardly had Leslie got rid of his than Mrs. Van Heldre was in the hall, her short plump arms were round Leslie's neck, and she kissed him heartily.

"God bless you!" she whispered with a sob; and before Leslie had well recovered from his surprise and confusion, Madelaine was holding one of his hands in both of hers, and looking tearfully in his face in a way which spoke volumes.

"Ah, it's nice to be young and good-looking, and well off," said Uncle Luke. "Nobody gives me such a welcome."

"How can you say that!" said Madelaine, with a laugh. "Come, Uncle Luke, and we're very glad to see you."

As she spoke she put her hands on his shoulders, and kissed his wrinkled cheek.

"Hah! that's like old times, Maddy," said the grim-looking visitor, softening a little.

" Why didn't you keep a nice plump little girl, same as you used to be ? "

Madelaine gave him a smile and nod but left the old man with her father, and followed her mother and Leslie into the dining-room.

" So that's to be it, is it, Van, eh ? "

" I don't know," was the reply. " It's all very sudden and a surprise to me."

" Angled for it, haven't you ? "

" Angled ? No."

" She has then. My dear boy, son of my heart, the very man for my darling, eh ? " chuckled Uncle Luke.

" Be quiet, you sham cynic," said Van Heldre dreamily. " Don't banter me, Luke, I'm sorely ill at ease."

" About money, eh ? " cried Uncle Luke eagerly.

" Money ? No ! I was thinking about those poor fellows out at sea."

" In your brig, eh ? Ah, 'tis sad. But that money—quite safe, eh ? "

" Oh yes, safe enough."

" Oh, do come, papa dear," said Madelaine, reappearing at the door. " Dinner is waiting."

" Yes, yes, we're coming, my dear," said Van Heldre, laying his hand affectionately on

Uncle Luke's shoulder, and they were soon after seated round the table, with the elder visitor showing at times quite another side of his character.

No allusion was made to the adventure of the morning, but Leslie felt in the gentle tenderness displayed towards him by mother and daughter that much had been said, and that he had won a very warm place in their regard. In fact, in word and look, Mrs. Van Heldre seemed to be giving him a home in her motherly heart, which was rather embarrassing, and would have been more so, but for Madelaine's frank, pleasant way of meeting his gaze, every action seemed to be sisterly and affectionate but nothing more.

So Leslie read them, but so did not the elders at the table.

By mutual consent no allusion was made to the missing brig, and it seemed to Leslie that the thoughts of mother and daughter were directed principally to one point, that of diverting Van Heldre from his troublesome thoughts.

"Ah, I was hungry," said Uncle Luke, when the repast was about half over. "Very pleasant meal, only wanted one thing to make it perfect."

238 OF HIGH DESCENT.

"Why, my dear Luke Vine, why didn't you speak? What is it? oh, pray say."

"Society," said Uncle Luke, after pausing for a moment to turn towards the window, a gust having given it a tremendous shake. "I say, if I find my place blown away, can you find me a dry shed or a dog kennel or something, Leslie?"

"Don't talk such stuff, Luke Vine," cried Mrs. Van Heldre. "Don't take any notice of him, Mr. Leslie, he's a rich old miser and nothing else. Now, Luke Vine, what do you mean?"

"Said what I meant, society. Why didn't you ask my sister to dinner? She'd have set us all right, eh, Madelaine?"

"Oh, I don't know," said Madelaine, smiling.

"But I do," cried her mother; "she'd have set us all by the ears with her nonsense. You are a strange pair."

"We are—we are. Nice sherry this, Van."

"Glad you like it," said Van Heldre, with his eyes turned towards the window, as if he expected news.

"How a woman can be so full of pride and so useless puzzles me."

"Mamma!" whispered Madelaine, with an imploring look.

"Let her talk, my dear," said Uncle Luke, "it doesn't hurt any one. Don't talk nonsense, Van's wife. What use could you make of her? She is like the thistle that grows up behind my place, a good-looking prickly plant, with a ball of down for a head. Let her be; you always get the worst of it. The more you excite her the more that head of hers sends out floating downy seeds to settle here and there and do mischief. She has spoiled my nephew Harry, and nearly spoiled my niece."

"Don't you believe it, Mr. Leslie," cried Madelaine, with a long earnest look in her eyes.

"Quite true, Miss Impudence," continued Uncle Luke. "Always was a war between me and the useless plants."

"Well, I can't sit here silent and listen to such heresy," cried Mrs. Van Heldre, shaking her head. "Surely, Luke Vine, you don't call yourself a useful plant."

"Bless my soul, ma'am, then I suppose I'm a weed?"

"Not you," said Van Heldre, forcing a show of interest in the conversation.

"Yes, old fellow, I am," said Uncle Luke, holding his sherry up to the light, and sipping

it as if he found real enjoyment therein. " I
suppose I am only a weed, not a thistle, like
Margaret up yonder, but a tough-rooted,
stringy, matter-of fact old nettle, who comes
up quietly in his own corner, and injures no
one so long as people let him alone."

" No, no, no, no!" said Madelaine emphatically.

" Quite right, Miss Van Heldre," said Leslie.

" Hear, hear!" cried Van Heldre.

" Stir me up, then, and see," cried the old
man grimly. " More than one person has
found out before now how I can sting, and—
Hallo! what's wrong? You here?"

There had been a quick step in the long
passage, and, without ceremony, the door
was thrown open, Harry Vine entering, to
stand in the gathering gloom hatless and
excited.

He was about to speak, Van Heldre having
sprung to his feet, when the young man's eyes
alighted on Leslie and Madelaine seated side
by side at the table, and the flash of anger
which mounted to his brain drove everything
else away.

" What is it?" cried Van Heldre hoarsely.
" Do you hear?—speak!"

" There is a brig on the Conger Rock," said

Harry quickly, as if roused to a recollection of that which he had come to say.

"Yes, sir," cried another voice, as old Crampton suddenly appeared. "And the man has just run up to the office with the news, for——"

"Well, man, speak out," said Van Heldre, whose florid face was mottled with patches of ghastly white.

"They think it's ours."

"I felt it coming," groaned Van Heldre, as he rushed into the hall, Leslie following quickly.

As he hurriedly threw on his waterproof a hand caught his, and turning, it was to see Madelaine looking up imploringly in his eyes.

"My father, Mr. Leslie. Keep him out of danger, pray!"

"Trust me. I'll do my best," said the young man quickly; and then he awoke to the fact that Harry Vine was beside him, white with anger, an anger which seemed to make him dumb.

The next minute the whole party were struggling down the street against the hurricane-like wind, to learn from a dozen voices, eager to tender the bad news, that the mist of spray had been so thick that in the early gloom of evening the vessel had approached quite unseen till she was close in, and directly after she had struck on the dangerous rock, in a wild attempt to reach the harbour, a task next to impossible in such a storm.

# CHAPTER XVIII.

## HARRY VINE SHOWS HIS BRIGHT SIDE.

THE wreck of a ship on the threshold of
the home where every occupant is known, is a
scene of excitement beyond the reach of pen
to adequately describe ; and as the two young
men reached the mouth of the harbour, following closely upon Van Heldre, their own
petty animosity was forgotten in the face of
the terrible disaster.

The night was coming fast, and a light had
been hoisted in the rigging of the vessel, now
hard on the dangerous rock—the long arc of
a circle described by the dim star showing
plainly to those on shore the precarious position of the unfortunate crew.

The sides of the harbour were crowded, in
spite of the tremendous storm of wind and
spray ; and, as Leslie followed the ship-owner,
he noted the horror and despair in many a
spray-wet face.

R 2

As Van Heldre approached and was recognized there was a cheer given by those who seemed to take it for granted that the owner would at once devise a way to save the vessel from her perilous position ; and rescue the crew whose lives were dear to many gathered in agony around, to see, as it were, their dear ones die.

Steps had already been taken, however, and as the little party from Van Heldre's reached the harbour it was to see the life-boat launched, and a crew of sturdy fellows in their places, ready to do battle with the waves.

It seemed to be a terrible task to row right out from the comparatively calm harbour, whose long rocky point acted as a breakwater, to where the great billows came rolling in, each looking as if it would engulf a score of such frail craft as that which, after a little of the hesitation of preparation, and amidst a tremendous burst of cheering, was rowed out into the middle of the estuary, and then straight away for the mouth.

But they were not all cheers which followed the boat. Close by where Leslie stood, with a choking sensation of emotion in his breast, a woman uttered a wild shriek as the boat went off, and her hands were outstretched towards one of the oilskin-cased men, who sat in his place tugging stolidly at his oar.

That one cry, heard above the roaring of the wind, the hiss of the spray, and the heavy thunder of the waves, acted like a signal to let loose the pent-up agony of a score of hearts ; and wives, mothers, sisters, all joined in that one wild cry, " Come back ! "

The answer was a hoarse " Give way ! " from the coxswain ; and the crew turned their eyes determinedly from the harbour wall and tugged at their oars.

The progress of the boat was followed as far as was possible by the crowd ; and when they could go no farther, every sheltered spot was seized upon as a coign of vantage from which to watch the saving of the doomed crew.

Leslie was standing close to the harbour wall, sheltering his face with his hands as he watched the life-boat fast nearing the mouth of the harbour, where the tug of war would commence, when he felt a hand laid upon his arm.

He turned sharply, to find Madelaine at his elbow, her hood drawn over her head and tightly secured beneath her chin.

He hardly saw her face, though, for close beside her stood another closely-hooded figure, whose face was streaming with the spray, while strand after strand of her dark hair had been torn from its place by the wind, and refused to be controlled.

"Miss Van Heldre! Miss Vine!"

" Yes. Where is my father?"

" Here; talking to this coastguardsman."

" And I thought we had lost him," murmured Madelaine.

" But is it wise of you two ladies?" said Leslie, as he grasped Louise's hand for a moment. " The storm is too terrible."

" We could not rest indoors," said Louise. " My father is down here, is he not?"

" I have not seen him. You want some better shelter."

" No, no; don't think of us," said Louise excitedly; " but if you can help in any way——"

" You know I will," said Leslie earnestly.

" Here, what are you two girls doing?" said a quick, angry voice. " Louie, I'm sure this is no place for you."

Harry spoke to his sister, but his eyes were fixed upon those of Leslie, who, however, declined his challenge, as it seemed, to quarrel, and glanced at the young man's companion.

At that moment the brothers Vine came up,

and there was no farther excuse for Harry's fault-finding objections.

" Can't you young fellows do anything to help ? " said Uncle Luke.

" I wish you would tell us what to do, Mr. Vine," said Leslie coldly.

Just then Van Heldre turned to, and joined them.

" He is afraid the distance is too far," he said dreamily, as if in answer to a question. .

" For the boat, Mr. Van Heldre ? " cried Louise.

" No, no ; for the rocket apparatus. Ah ! Vine," he continued, as he saw his old friend, " how helpless we are in such a storm ! "

No more was said. It was no time for words. The members of the two families stood together in a group watching the progress of the boat, and even Aunt Marguerite's cold and sluggish blood was moved enough to draw her to the window, through whose spray and salt-blurred panes she could dimly see the tossing light of the brig.

It was indeed no time for words, and even the very breath was held, to be allowed to escape in a low hiss of exultation as the lifeboat was seen to rise suddenly and swiftly up a great bank of water, stand out upon its

summit for a few moments, and then plunge
down out of sight as the wave came on, deluged
the point, and roared and tumbled over in the
mouth of the harbour.

It was plain enough now; the life-boat was
beyond the protection of the point; and its
progress was watched as it rose and fell, slowly
growing more distant, and at times invisible
for minutes together.

At such times the excitement seemed
beyond bearing. The boat, all felt, must
have been swamped, and those on board left
tossing in the boiling sea. The catastrophe
of the wreck of the brig seemed to be swal-
lowed up now in one that was greater; and
as Leslie glanced round once, it was to see
Louise and Madelaine clinging together, wild-
eyed and pale.

"There she is!" shouted a voice; and the
life-boat was seen to slowly rise again, as a
hoarse cheer arose—the pent-up excitement of
the moment.

It seemed an interminable length of time
before the life-saving vessel reached the brig,
and what followed during the next half-hour
could only be guessed at. So dark had it
become that now only the tossing light on
board the doomed merchantman could be seen,

rising and falling slowly with rhythmical regularity, as if those on board were waving to those they loved a sad farewell.

Then at last a faint spark was seen for a few moments before it disappeared. Again it shone for a while and again disappeared.

" One of the lanthorns in the life-boat."

"Coming back," said Van Heldre hoarsely.

" With the crew, sir ? " cried Leslie.

" Hah ! " exclaimed Van Heldre slowly; "that we must see."

Another long time of suspense and horror. A dozen times over that boat's light seemed to have gone for ever, but only to reappear; and at last, in the darkness it was seen, after a few minutes' tremendous tossing, to become steady.

The life-boat was in the harbour once again, and a ringing burst of cheers, that seemed smothered directly after by the roar of the storm, greeted the crew as they rowed up to the landing-place, utterly exhausted, but bringing with them two half-dead members of the brig's crew.

" All we could get to stir," said the sturdy coxswain, " and we could not get aboard."

" How many are there ? "

" Seven, sir—in main-top.  Half dead."

"You should have stayed and brought them off," cried Leslie frantically, for he did not realize the difficulties of the task the men had had to fulfil.

"Who goes next?" cried Van Heldre, as the half-drowned men were borne, under the direction of the doctor, to the nearest inn.

"No one can't go again, sir," said the old coxswain sternly. "It arn't to be done."

"A crew must go again," cried Van Heldre. "We cannot stand here and let them perish before our eyes. Here, my lads!" he roared. "Volunteers!"

"Mr. Leslie! My father," whispered Madelaine; but the young mine-owner was already on his way to where Van Heldre stood.

"Do you hear?" roared the latter. "Do as you would be done by. Volunteers!"

Not a man stirred, the peril was too great.

"It's no good, master," said the old coxswain; "they're gone, poor lads, by now."

"No," cried Leslie excitedly; "the light is there still."

"Ay," said the coxswain, "a lamp 'll burn some time longer than a man's life. Here, master, I'll go again, if you can get a crew."

"Volunteers!" shouted Van Heldre, but there was only a confused babble of voices, as women clung to their men and held back those who would have yielded.

"Are you men!" roared Leslie excitedly; and Madelaine felt her arm grasped tightly. "I say, are you men, to stand there and see those poor fellows perish before your eyes!"

"It's throwing lives away," cried a shrill woman's voice.

"Ay, go yoursen," shouted a man angrily.

"I'm going," roared Leslie. "Only a landsman. Now then, is there never a sailor who will come?"

There was a panting, spasmodic cry at Madelaine's ear, one which she echoed, as Harry Vine stepped up to Leslie's side.

"Here's another landsman," he cried excitedly. "Now, Pradelle, come on!"

There was no response from his companion, who drew back.

"No, no," panted Madelaine. "Louie— help me—they must not go."

Her words were drowned in a tremendous cheer, for Van Heldre, without a word, had stepped into the life-boat, followed by the two young men.

Example is said to be better than precept. It was so here, for, with a rush, twenty of the sturdy Hakemouth fishers made for the boat, and the crew was not only made up, but a dozen men begged Van Heldre and the two young men to come out and let others take their places.

"No," said Leslie through his set teeth; "not if I never see shore again, Henry Vine."

"Is that brag to Hector over me, or British pluck?" said Harry.

"Don't know, my lad. Are you going ashore?"

"Let's wait and see," muttered Harry, as he tied on the life-preserver handed to him.

"Harry, my boy!"

The young man looked up and saw his father on the harbour wall.

"Hallo! Father!" he said sadly.

"You are too young and weak. Let some strong man go."

"I can pull an oar as well as most of them, father," he shouted; and then to himself: "And if I don't get back—well—I suppose I'm not much good."

"Let him go," said Uncle Luke, as he held back his brother. "Hang the boy, he has stuff in him after all."

A busy scene of confusion for a few minutes, and then once more a cheer arose, as the life-boat, well manned, parted the waters of the harbour, and the lanthorns forward and astern shone with a dull glare as that first great wave was reached, up which the boat glided, and then plunged down and disappeared.

One long hour of intense agony, but not for those in the boat. The energy called forth, the tremendous struggle, the excitement to which every spirit was wrought, kept off agony or fear. It was like being in the supreme moments of a battle-charge, when in the wild whirl there is no room for dread, and a man's spirit carries him through to the end.

The agony was on shore, where women clung together no longer weeping, but straining their eyes seaward for the dancing lights which dimly crept up each billow, and then disappeared, as if never to appear again.

"Madelaine!"

"Louise!"

All that was said as the two girls clasped each other and watched the dim lanthorns far at sea.

"Ah!"

Then a loud groan.

"I knowed it couldn't be long."

Then another deep murmur, whose strange intensity had made it dominate the shrieks, roars, and thunder of the storm.

The light, which had been slowly waving up and down in the rigging of the brig, had disappeared, and it told to all the sad tale—that the mast had gone, and with it those who had been clinging in the top.

But the two dim lanthorns in the life-boat went on and on, the thunder of the surf on the wreck guiding them. As the crew toiled away, the landsmen sufficiently accustomed to the use of the oar could pretty well hold their own, till, in utter despair and hopelessness, after hovering hours about the place where the wreck should have been, the life-boat's head was laid for the harbour lights; and after a fierce battle to avoid being driven beyond, the gallant little crew reached the shelter given by the long low point, but several had almost to be lifted to the wharf.

A few jagged and torn timbers, and a couple of bodies cast up among the rocks, a couple of miles to the east, were all the traces of Van Heldre's handsome brig, which had gone to pieces in the darkness before the life-boat, on its second journey, was half-way there.

# CHAPTER XIX.

## A BAD NIGHT'S WORK.

"Oh, yes, you're a very brave fellow, no doubt," said Pradelle. "Everybody says so. Perhaps if I could have handled an oar as well as you did I should have come too. But look here, Harry Vine; all these find words butter no parsnips. You are no better off than you were before, and you gave me your promise."

It was quite true: fine words buttered no parsnips. Aunt Marguerite had called him her gallant young hero; Louise had kissed him affectionately; his father had shaken hands very warmly; Uncle Luke had given him a nod, and Van Heldre had said a few kindly words, while there was always a smile for him among the fishermen who hung about the harbour. But that was all; he was still Van Heldre's clerk, and with a dislike to his position, which had become intensified since

Madelaine had grown cold, and her intimacy with Leslie had seemed to increase.

"Look here," said Pradelle; "it's time I was off."

"Why? What for?" said Harry, as they sat among the rocks.

"Because I feel as if I were being made a fool."

"Why, every one is as civil to you as can be. My father——"

"Oh, yes; the old man's right enough."

"My aunt."

"Yes, wish she wasn't so old, Harry, and had some money; I'd marry her."

"Don't be a fool."

"Not going to be; so I tell you I'm off."

"No, no, don't go. This place will be unbearable when you are gone."

"Can't help it, dear boy. I must do something to increase my income, and if you will not join in and make a fortune, why I must go and find some one who will."

"But I dare not, Vic."

"You gave me your word—the word of a gentleman. I ask you to borrow the money for a week or two, and then we would replace it, and nobody be a bit the wiser, while we shall be on the high-road to fortune and fair France."

"I tell you I dare not."

"Then I shall do it myself."

"No, that you shall not."

"Then you shall."

"I daren't."

"Bah! what a milksop you are; you have nothing to care for here. Miss Van Heldre has pitched you over because you are now her father's clerk."

"Let that be, please."

"And taken up with Mr. Bagpipes."

"Do you want to quarrel, Pradelle?"

"Not I, dear boy; I'm dumb."

He said no more on that subject, but he had said enough. That was the truth then. Madelaine had given him up on that account, and the sting rankled in Harry's breast.

"Money goes to the bank every day, you say?" said Pradelle.

"Yes. Crampton takes it."

"But that sum of money in notes? How much is there of that?"

"Five hundred."

"Why don't that go to the bank?"

"I don't know. A deposit, I think; likely to be called for."

"May be; but that's our game, Harry. The

other could not be managed without being missed; this, you see, is not in use."

"Pradelle, it's madness."

"Say Vic, dear boy."

"Well, Vic, I say it's madness."

"Nothing of the kind. It's making use of a little coin that you can get at easily. Why, hang it, old fellow, you talk as if I were asking you to steal the money."

"Hush! Don't talk like that."

"Well, you aggravate me so. Now, am I trying to serve you, or am I not?"

"To serve me, of course."

"Yes, and you behave like a child."

"I want to behave like an honourable man to my father's friend."

"Oh, if you are going to preach I'm off."

"I'm not going to preach."

"Then do act like a man. Here is your opportunity. You know what the old chap said about the tide in the affairs of men?"

Harry nodded.

"Well, your tide is at its height. You are going to seize your opportunity, and then you can do as you like. Why you might turn the tables on Miss Madelaine."

"If you don't want to quarrel just leave

her name alone," said Harry, with a bulldog-like growl.

" Oh, I'll never mention it again if you like. Now, then, once for all, is it business ?"

Harry was silent for a few minutes, and then replied—

" Yes."

" Your hand on it."

Harry stretched out his hand unwillingly, and it was taken and held.

" I shall hold you to it now, my lad. Now, then, when is it to be ?"

" Oh, first opportunity."

" No ; it's going to be now—to-night—as soon as it's dark."

" Nonsense, it must be some day—when Crampton is not there."

" That means it will not be done at all, for Crampton never leaves ; you told me so. Look here, Harry Vine, if you borrow the amount then, and it's missed, of course you are asked directly, and there you are. No, my lad, you'll have to go to-night."

" But it will be like housebreaking."

" Bah ! You'll go quietly in by the back way, make your way along the passage to Van Heldre's room, take the keys down from the hook——"

"How did you know that the keys hung there?"

"Because, my dear little man, I have wormed it all out of you by degrees. To continue; you will go down the glass passage, open the office door, go to the safe, open that, get the two hundred——"

"Two hundred! You said fifty would do."

"Yes, but then I said a hundred, and now I think two will be better. Easier paid back. You can work more spiritedly with large sums than with small. You've got to do this, Harry Vine, so no nonsense."

Harry was silent.

"When you have the notes, you will lock all up as before, and then if they are missing before we return them, which is not likely, who can say that you have been there? Bah! don't be so squeamish. You've got to do that to-night. You have promised, and you shall. It is for your good, my lad."

"Yes, and yours," said Harry gloomily.

"Of course. Emancipation for us both."

Harry was silent, and soon after they rose and strolled back to the old house, where through the open window came the strains of music, and the voices of Madelaine and Louise harmonized in a duet.

"One less at Van Heldre's, lad. The old man will be having his evening pipe, and the doors open. Nothing could be better. Half-past nine, mind, while they are at tea. It will be quite dark then."

Harry was silent, and the two young men entered and sat down, their coming seeming to cast a damp on the little party, for the music was put aside and work taken up, Vine being busy with some notes of his day's observations of the actions of a newly-found mollusc.

Tea was brought in at about a quarter past nine, and Pradelle rose and went to the window.

"What a beautiful night, Harry," he said. "Coming for half an hour's stroll before bed?"

"Don't you want some tea?" said Harry, loudly.

"No. Do you?"

"No," said Harry shortly; and he rose and went out, followed by his friend.

"You mean this then," he said, as soon as they were out on the cliff.

"No; but you do. There is just time for it, so now go."

Harry hesitated for a few minutes, and then

strode off down toward the town, Pradelle keeping step with him, till they reached the street where a lane branched off, going round by the back of Van Heldre's house, but on a higher level, a flight of steps leading down into the half garden, half yard, overlooked by the houses at the back, whose basements were level with Van Heldre's first floor.

The time selected by Pradelle for the carrying out of his scheme happened to be Crampton's club night, and, according to his weekly custom, he had gone to the old-fashioned inn where it was kept, passing a muffled-up figure as he went along, the said figure turning in at one of the low entrances leading to dock premises as the old clerk came out, so that he did not see the face.

It was a trifling matter, but it was not the first time Crampton had seen this figure loitering about at night, and it somehow impressed him so that he did not enjoy his one glass of spirits and water and his pipe. But the matter seemed to have slipped his memory for the time that he was transacting his club business, making entries and the like. Later on it came back with renewed force.

Harry and Pradelle parted in the dark lane with very few more words spoken, the under-

standing being that they should meet at home
at half-past nine.

As soon as the former was alone, he walked
slowly on round the front of Van Heldre's
house, and there, according to custom, sat the
merchant, smoking his nightly pipe, resting
one arm upon the table, with the shaded lamp
shining down on his bald forehead, and a
thoughtful, dreamy look in his eyes. Mrs.
Van Heldre was seated opposite, working and
respecting her husband's thoughtful mood, for
he was in low spirits respecting the wreck of
his ship. Insurance made up the monetary
loss, but nothing could restore the poor fellows
who had gone down.

Harry stood on the opposite side, watching
thoughtfully.

"It would be very easy," he said to himself. "Just as we planned, I can slip round
to the back, drop in the garden, go in, take
the keys, get the money, lock up again, and
go and hang up the keys. Yes; how easy for
any one who knows, and how risky it seems
for him to leave his place like that. But then
it is people's want of knowledge which forms
the safest lock."

"Yes," he said, after a pause, as he stood
there in profound ignorance of the fact that

the muffled-up figure which had taken Crampton's attention was in a low dark doorway,
watching his every movement. "Yes; it would
be very easy; and in spite of all your precious
gloss, Master Victor Pradelle, I should feel the
next moment that I had been a thief; and I'll
drudge as a clerk till I'm ninety-nine before
I'll do anything of the kind."

He thrust his hands into his pockets and
turned off down by the harbour side, and
hardly had he reached the water when Pradelle walked slowly up to the front of the
house, noted the positions of those within by
taking his stand just beneath the arched doorway opposite, and so close to the watcher that
they nearly touched.

The next moment Pradelle had passed on.

"I knew he hadn't the pluck," he muttered
bitterly. "A contemptible hound! Well, he
shall see."

Without a moment's hesitation, and as if he
were quite at home about the place, Pradelle
went round to the narrow back lane and stood
by the gate leading down the steps into the
yard. As he pressed the gate it gave way,
and he could see that the doorway into the
glazed passage was open, for the light in the
hall shone through.

There was no difficulty at all; and after a moment's hesitation he stepped lightly down, ready with an excuse that he was seeking Harry, if he should meet any one; but the excuse was not needed. He walked softly and boldly into the passage, turned to his right, and entered the back room, which acted as Van Heldre's private office and study. The keys lay where he knew them to be—in a drawer, which he opened and took them out, and then walked straight along the glazed passage to the office. The door yielded to the key, and he entered. The inner office was locked, but that was opened by a second key, and the safe showed dimly by the reflected lights which shone through the barred window.

"How easy these things are!" said Pradelle to himself, as he unlocked the safe; "enough to tempt a man to be a burglar."

The iron door creaked faintly as he drew it open, and then began to feel about hastily, and with the perspiration streaming from his forehead. Books in plenty, but no notes.

With an exclamation of impatience, he drew out a little match-box, struck a light, and saw that there was an iron drawer low down. The flame went out, but he had seen enough, and stooping he dragged out the drawer, thrust in his hand, which came in contact with a leaden paper weight, beneath which, tied round with tape, was a bundle of notes.

"Hah!" he muttered with a half laugh, "I can't stop to count you. Yes, I must, or they'll miss 'em. It's tempting though. Humph! tied both——"

*Thud!*

One heavy blow on the back of Victor Pradelle's head which sent him staggering forward against the door of the safe; then he felt in a confused, half-stunned way that something had been snatched from his hand. A dead silence followed, during which his head swam, but he had sufficient sense left to totter across the outer office, and along the passage to the garden yard.

How he got outside into the little lane he could not afterwards remember, his next recollection being of sitting down on the steps by the water-side bathing his face.

Five minutes before Harry Vine had been in that very spot, from which he turned to go home.

"Let him say what he likes," muttered the young man; "I must have been mad to listen to him. Why——"

Harry Vine stopped short, for a thought had struck him like a flash.

How it was—why he should have such a suspicion he could not tell; but a terrible thought had seemed to burn into his brain. Then he felt paralyzed as he shivered, and uttering an ejaculation full of rage and anger, he started off at a run towards Van Heldre's place.

"Nonsense!" he said to himself, and he checked his headlong speed. "What folly!"

He walked on past a group of seamen, who had just quitted a public-house, and was about to turn up the lane which led to his home, when the thought came once more.

"Curse him!" he said, half aloud, "I'd sooner kill him," and hurrying back, he made straight for the lane behind Van Heldre's.

The gate yielded, he stepped down quickly into the yard, walked to the open door, looked to the right toward the hall, and then to the left toward the office. A dim light shone down the passage, and his heart seemed to stand still. The office door was open, and without hesitation he turned down the passage panting with horror, as he felt that his suspicions were confirmed. He crossed the outer room, the inner door was shut, and entering he paused for a moment.

"Vic!" he whispered harshly.

All was still.

Trembling now with agitation, he was rapidly crossing to the safe when he stepped on something which gave beneath his feet, and he nearly fell headlong.

Recovering himself, he stooped down to pick up the heavy ebony ruler used by old Crampton, and polished by rubs of his coat-tail till it shone.

Harry felt giddy now with excitement, but he went to the safe door, felt that it was swung open, and groaning to himself, "Too late, too late!" he bent his head and felt for the drawer.

Empty!

"You scoundrel!" he groaned; "but he shall give up every note, and——"

Once more he felt as if paralyzed, for as he turned from the safe he knew that he was not alone in the office.

Caught in the act! Burglary—the open safe—the notes gone, who would believe in his innocency?

He could think of nothing else, as he heard

Van Heldre's voice in the darkness—one fierce angry utterance—" Who's there ? "

" He does not know me," flashed through Harry Vine's brain.

" You villain ! " cried Van Heldre, springing at him.

It was the instinctive act of one smitten by terror, despair, shame, and the desire to escape — a mad act, but prompted by the terrible position. As Van Heldre sprang at him and grasped at his breast, Harry Vine struck with all his might, the heavy ruler fell with a sickening crash upon the unguarded head, he felt a sudden tug, and with a groan his father's friend sank senseless on the floor.

For one moment Harry Vine stood bending over his victim; then uttering a hoarse sigh, he leaped over the body and fled.

END OF VOLUME I.

www.ingramcontent.com/pod-product-compliance
Lightning Source LLC
Chambersburg PA
CBHW020346030726
47496CB00007B/2019